Her head cocked and her eyes narrowed. "You know a lot about me and my family."

"I made it my business." He squared his shoulders and met her gaze directly. "I guess my ten minutes are up now. Do I stay or go?"

She was silent a moment before finally giving a single backward jerk of her head and turning toward the house.

As she started up the steps, he let himself into the yard and closed the gate behind him, pausing a moment to let Patton greet him properly. He looked up to find Megan watching him from the open doorway. She'd tucked the phone in the pocket of her running shorts, but the shotgun remained in her hand.

In an instant, he felt a tug low in his belly, an attraction to this backwoods avenging angel, with her fiery hair, stormy eyes and death at her fingertips.

She was dangerous on an entirely different level.

PAULA GRAVES

SECRET AGENDA

Harlequin®

TORONTO NEW YORK LONDON
AMSTERDAM PARIS SYDNEY HAMBURG
STOCKHOLM ATHENS TOKYO MILAN MADRID
PRAGUE WARSAW BUDAPEST AUCKLAND

For the hardworking, hard-fighting men and women of the U.S. Armed Forces, with my heartfelt gratitude for your service. You give true meaning to the word *hero*.

ISBN-13: 978-0-373-74669-9

SECRET AGENDA

Copyright © 2012 by Paula Graves

ABOUT THE AUTHOR

Alabama native Paula Graves wrote her first book, a mystery starring herself and her neighborhood friends, at the age of six. A voracious reader, Paula loves books that pair tantalizing mystery with compelling romance. When she's not reading or writing, she works as a creative director for a Birmingham advertising agency and spends time with her family and friends. She is a member of Southern Magic Romance Writers, Heart of Dixie Romance Writers and Romance Writers of America. Paula invites readers to visit her website, www.paulagraves.com.

Books by Paula Graves

HARLEQUIN INTRIGUE

926—FORBIDDEN TERRITORY
998—FORBIDDEN TEMPTATION
1046—FORBIDDEN TOUCH
1088—COWBOY ALIBI
1183—CASE FILE: CANYON CREEK, WYOMING*
1189—CHICKASAW COUNTY CAPTIVE*
1224—ONE TOUGH MARINE*
1230—BACHELOR SHERIFF*
1272—HITCHED AND HUNTED**
1278—THE MAN FROM GOSSAMER RIDGE**
1285—COOPER VENGEANCE**
1305—MAJOR NANNY
1337—SECRET IDENTITY†
1342—SECRET HIDEOUT†
1348—SECRET AGENDA†

*Cooper Justice
**Cooper Justice: Cold Case Investigation
†Cooper Security

CAST OF CHARACTERS

Megan Randall—Four years a widow, Megan Randall still blames her husband's war-zone death on too-restrictive rules of engagement enforced by Pentagon lawyer Evan Pike. When Pike shows up on her doorstep, claiming her husband was murdered by rogue mercenaries, how can she believe him?

Evan Pike—Driven by his own sense of guilt and a passion for justice, Pike needs to convince Vince Randall's widow that the soldier's letters home may hold a clue to his killer. But he doesn't expect to find himself so attracted to the feisty widow.

Vince Randall—Megan's late husband was an army sergeant willing to lay his life on the line for his fellow soldiers. But was his death on a peacekeeping mission really a casualty of war? Or was there a darker conspiracy behind it?

Jesse Cooper—Megan's brother owns Cooper Security and has his own reasons for wanting to hunt down the mercenaries Pike believes are behind his brother-in-law's death. But is he willing to allow his sister to put her life on the line, as well?

Donald Gates—The former soldier was tasked with sending Megan a package from her husband, a package that never arrived. Could he have been involved in Vince's murder?

Security Services Unit (SSU)—MacLear Security's secret unit disbanded when the company fell to scandal. But some of the operatives are still selling their services to whoever's willing to pay. Were they behind Vince Randall's death?

Elmore Gantry—Vince Randall's former captain may know more about Vince's death than he's telling. But will Megan's attempt to confront the officer put her life in even graver danger?

Scott Merriwether—The soldier had carried a message to Vince's unit shortly before Vince was killed. Now he's dead in a suspicious accident. Could his death be connected to the mystery?

Chapter One

Megan Randall dusted aside the fallen leaves and twigs scattered across the gravestone, detritus of the storm that had blown through northeastern Alabama overnight. She never put flowers on her husband's grave, not even on decoration day. Soft had never been his style. Vince had been tough as old leather, strong as steel. She'd loved that part of him since she was sixteen. She wouldn't dishonor it after death.

Of course, he'd hate to know she visited his grave daily, like a ritual, but he'd just have to forgive her.

"No tornadoes this time." She traced the curves and lines of his name etched in the glossy granite. "A limb from the hickory tree in the backyard fell on my tomatoes, though. Ticked me off."

The only answer was a light breeze rustling the trees nearby and the soft snuffling sound of Patton investigating the grass behind her. He tugged impatiently on the leash, a signal to move along before he did something they'd both regret on one of the nearby graves.

She led the mutt out of the small graveyard, sparing a quick look behind her as they moved back onto the country road. Vince could have qualified for burial with honors at Arlington, but he'd made her promise that if he died in battle, she'd lay him to rest right here in Chickasaw County. He was an Alabama boy, born and bred.

Patton pulled to a halt, his normally floppy ears peaked and his furry body rigidly at attention. He gazed into the woods ahead, a low whine emerging from his throat. Not a warning, exactly, but it made the hair on the back of Megan's neck prickle.

She peered into the gloom, unable to see any movement within the thick vegetation. A squirrel, she thought. Or a rabbit. Nothing more threatening than that.

But the hair on the back of her neck continued to rise.

Though not a fearful person, Megan wasn't foolish. Her house was only a mile up the road, but Patton's soft whines convinced her to circle back around the cemetery toward her sister's house and the safety of numbers. It was Saturday morning, so Isabel and Ben would probably be home. And if they weren't, Megan had a key to let herself into the house.

To her surprise, however, Patton pulled against

the leash as she tried to bring him around in the opposite direction.

"Come on, Patton—let's go! Heel!" She gave a sharp tug, and the big dog finally came to heel as she'd trained him to do. He trotted beside her as she jogged toward her sister's house, his furry head turning now and then toward the direction from which they'd come.

She found Isabel and Ben in the front yard of the sprawling farmhouse, piling up limbs the storm had knocked from one of their old oaks. Patton tugged on the leash, eager to go to Isabel, one of his favorite people.

Megan's sister looked up at his happy bark and grinned. "Patty McPatton!" she called as Megan reached down and released the dog from his leash. The mutt raced to Isabel, his back end dancing as she bent to greet him.

Ben kept his distance—Patton was still deciding if he liked the new person taking up his beloved Isabel's attention—and smiled at Megan as she approached. "One of these days, that tree's going to come crashing down on the house. I keep telling Isabel we need to top it off, but I think it'd break her heart."

"What brings y'all here?" Isabel asked, still scratching Patton's ears while the dog panted.

Not wanting to admit she'd been spooked by a whining dog, Megan shrugged. "Just out for a run and thought we'd come by."

"Have you eaten yet?" Isabel asked. "Ben and I are about to drive to town for breakfast, as soon as we wash up. Want to join us? We can drop off Patton on the way."

Megan was sure the last thing the newlyweds needed was a third wheel for their breakfast date. "I've eaten," she lied. "But Patton and I will take a ride back to the house, if you're offering."

"Sure thing," Ben agreed. "Be right back."

"We'll be out here." Megan settled on the porch swing to wait, gazing toward the woods that lined the other side of the road. She still felt a low level sense of alarm, as if someone lurked in the deep woods, just out of her sight.

Someone watching her.

At her knee, Patton whined again, his tail thumping a steady cadence on the porch floor. Ears alert, he peered into the woods across the road.

Her heartbeat quickened. "What do you see, boy?"

The front door screen opened with a creak, making her jump. Isabel and Ben emerged, hand in hand. Megan tamped down a twinge of envy and greeted them with a smile.

"Sure you don't want to go to breakfast with us?" Ben asked. "You're more than welcome."

"I figure you two have at least three more months of matrimonial bliss before you'll really notice anyone else in the room with you, so I'll pass," she answered with genuine affection. Isabel and Ben had reunited only a month ago, after her sister had spent six months believing the man she secretly loved had been killed in a bomb explosion. She'd been given a second chance at love and grabbed it with both hands.

Megan would never get that chance. She'd seen her husband's body with her own eyes, still and lifeless in his dress blues. She'd said her goodbyes alone by his casket at the tiny church where he'd been baptized as a teenager. At least the kill shot had been through the heart, giving her the chance for an open casket and a final goodbye. She knew plenty of military widows who hadn't been afforded that.

It was a comfort, however small.

Patton piled into the backseat of Ben's Jeep Cherokee with Megan, snuggling close to her. He'd been here in the States with her for four years, since just before Vince's death, but he still got nervous in cars.

"How's he doing?" Isabel asked, meeting Megan's gaze in the rearview mirror.

"He's fine—aren't you, boy?" She gave the dog a hug and he leaned his muscular, furry body into hers. Tears stung her eyes but she fought them back.

He had been Vince's dog originally, a stray he and the other men in his squad had found wandering around their forward base in Ralijah, Kaziristan. He'd been a puppy, orphaned, perhaps, or just abandoned by his wandering mother. Young enough to tame easily under the affectionate care of his adopted family of soldiers, Patton had become the camp mascot. But after a scary near-miss with one of the unit's armored vehicles, Vince had arranged for the puppy to be shipped home to Megan.

She'd been happy for the companion and made fast friends with the German Shepherd mix puppy. They'd both waited patiently for three long months for Vince's return.

They hadn't expected he'd come home in a flag-draped box, she thought, her gaze drawn to her husband's gravesite as they passed the cemetery on the way to her house.

Ben and Isabel let her out at the front gate of her small bungalow, a river stone and clapboard house nestled in a wooded area near the base of Gossamer Mountain. A mile to the south, Gossamer Lake sparkled through the trees, reminding her that May was almost halfway over and she still hadn't been bluegill fishing with her cousin Hannah as promised.

She'd broken a lot of promises over the past four years.

"Come on, Patton, let's go inside." She unlocked the front door and waited for the dog to enter. But Patton lingered in the front yard, sniffing the monkey grass growing at the edge of the fence near the gate.

"Patton?"

He looked up at her briefly, panted happily, then resumed his investigation of the fence edge.

With a sigh, she entered the house alone, knowing he'd scratch at the door soon enough. Despite being a refugee from a very rugged land, he'd grown to appreciate the creature comforts of America, like central air-conditioning to ward off the humid heat of an Alabama summer and the dog food bowl that magically filled whenever he was hungry.

She wondered if he was still waiting for Vince to come home. Did he wonder why the big, tough soldier who saved him from a life of hardship had never shown up again?

Her eyes burned again. She rubbed her fingers against the sting until she regained control.

Today was May fourteenth. Seven years and a week ago, she'd married Vince Randall in the same little church where she'd laid him to rest. He was supposed to have come home in time to celebrate their third wedding anniversary.

Things hadn't worked out that way.

EVAN PIKE PARKED THE RENTED Ford Taurus on a narrow dirt turnabout just off Culpepper Road, pulling into the soft grass so that the car wouldn't easily be seen by passing vehicles. He didn't intend to hide his presence in Chickasaw County forever, but until he'd decided the best approach, he was inclined to keep a low profile.

Megan Randall lived a quarter mile down the road, in a single-story bungalow set back from the road behind a large chain-link fence. He knew this much because he'd already made a pass by the place earlier, not long after she and the dog had left for their morning walk. He'd looked around, just to get a feel for the kind of woman she might be.

The house itself had revealed little. Neat but not militant about it. Her life seemed simple and uncluttered. Plain house. Plain yard.

Only the woman herself was anything but plain, with her shock of wavy red hair and sleek, athletic body. He'd seen a photo of her once, tucked in Sergeant Randall's belongings after his death. More cute than pretty, with fair skin sprinkled with freckles and mysterious gray eyes.

The picture had done her no justice.

He'd caught up with her in person, unintentionally, a couple of miles down the road at a small cemetery next to a tiny stone church. Sergeant Randall's resting place, he'd guessed. He'd parked the rental car out of sight and went on foot through the woods across the road, keeping a careful distance as he watched the widow crouch at a grave and dust off a small marker.

The dog—Patton—had nearly seen him. He'd frozen in alarm as the dog started whining, a familiar sound he'd almost forgotten over the distance of four years.

When the woman and the dog had headed up the

road, he'd kept pace through the canopy of trees that hugged Old Maybridge Road as far as the eye could see.

After she'd stopped to speak with a man and woman in front of an old two-story farmhouse, Evan had lingered only a few minutes before retreating to where he'd left the car. Megan Randall had seemed intent to stay a while, giving him one more chance to take a look around her bungalow before she returned.

What he was looking for, he wasn't sure. An approach? A way to get through to her despite her obvious desire to keep her distance from anything reminding her of her husband's death?

She'd refused his initial request to meet with her. Blocked his subsequent calls. He'd even tried reaching her through Cooper Security, where she worked, only to learn she'd already warned her coworkers to refuse his calls.

A wise man would give up and go home. But nobody had accused Evan of being wise.

Not recently, anyway.

He had already reached the edge of her property when he saw movement inside the chain-link fence. Patton was snuffling a path along the long monkey grass planted at the edge of the fence. His head came up suddenly, his long nose sniffing the breeze. A low whine carried in the warm spring air, and Evan realized the dog had caught his scent.

He started to back away, but Patton caught sight of him and started barking a joyous greeting.

Seconds later, the front door opened and Megan Randall appeared in the opening, her hair released from the ponytail she'd worn while jogging. It spilled in russet waves over her shoulders, glistening in the morning sunlight. In her right hand she held a phone. In the left, a shotgun.

Evan's breath hitched as she caught sight of him, her gray eyes widening with surprise.

This might be his only chance to talk to her. All she could do was tell him to get lost, right?

Or shoot you.

He forced the words from his throat. "Mrs. Randall?"

Megan strode down the porch steps and stopped halfway to the gate. Her gaze slid from him to Patton, who stood on his back legs now, his front paws resting on the fence. His whole body wagged with joy, and Evan felt a powerful pull in the center of his chest, drawing him toward the animal.

"He's not friendly to strangers," Megan warned, but he heard doubt in her voice, as the dog's behavior was anything but threatening. "Neither am I," she added more confidently.

That he could believe.

Ignoring the tingle of danger at the back of his neck, Evan reached over the fence and rubbed the dog's jaw, allowing Patton to lick his hand. "Hey,

Patton. You're looking good, fellow! All grown up into a big, bad hound dog."

"Who are you?" Her voice was low and hard.

He met her gaze. "Evan Pike."

Her eyes iced over. "I told you I didn't want to talk to you about my husband."

He held his ground, despite the fierce anger in her expression. "I wouldn't be here if I didn't think what I have to tell you is something you need to know."

"I'm armed and you're trespassing. I don't know what you know about the laws here in Alabama, but they tend to be sympathetic to people protecting their property."

He arched an eyebrow. "You plan to shoot me? Really?"

"Are you sure I won't?" Like her husband, she had a hard-edged Southern drawl that reminded him of the place he'd once called home. He'd left Cumberland behind ages ago, but memories lingered, good and bad.

It had taken a couple of years back in Washington to regain his neutral inflections after two years in Kaziristan surrounded by a bunch of Southern boys in the army unit where he'd acted as a liaison to an Assistant Secretary of Defense, tasked with monitoring rules of engagement compliance after a politically embarrassing incident. He had to fight against lapsing into his native accent now as he spoke. "I need ten minutes of your time. If, when

I'm finished, you want me to leave, I'll go and not bother you again."

"I want you to go now."

"What are you afraid of, Mrs. Randall?" he countered. "You think I'm going to tell you something about your husband that you don't want to hear? I'm not."

Not yet, anyway.

"Funny. That's not what Vince thought."

So Vince had written home about him. He'd figured as much. It had taken over a year to get past Randall's native distrust of anyone from the civilian side of the Pentagon. His passion had been the safety of his men, and while he'd understood the need for limits in the rules of engagement, Vince Randall had seen too many deaths and even more close calls to be happy about limits on what his men could do to protect themselves.

Evan wondered, even now, to what lengths Randall might have gone to protect his men. What compromises he might have made.

"You don't look surprised," she said darkly.

"I know soldiers write home."

The ice melted under the anger burning in her eyes, lighting her up like a lantern, all hissing flames and pent-up energy. "I reckon they feel they ought to warn the folks who love them that someday, some well-meaning but out-of-touch lawyer from D.C. is going to get them all killed."

"I don't blame you for being angry—"

"You don't blame *me?*" She stared at him in disbelief, visibly bristling. "I blame *you.*" Her voice broke. "I blame you for four years of living alone without the man I loved practically my whole life. I blame you for the kids we'll never have and the house we'll never build together and—" Her voice broke, her face creasing with frustration.

He felt sick, but he couldn't stop now. This might be as close as he'd ever get to finding out what really happened that night in Mi'Qaa Valley. "I understand your feelings—"

"Don't handle me," she warned, the hand with the shotgun lifting in warning.

Patton whimpered softly, as if sensing the sudden miasma of tension roiling across the yard between them.

He held up his hands in surrender. "I'm not. But I have to tell you something you need to know, even if you don't want to hear it." He didn't let her interrupt, though he could see the intention shining in her stormy eyes. "I don't think al Adar rebels killed your husband."

Her eyebrows arched. "What?"

Even as he opened his mouth to speak, the words stuck in his throat. How sure was he, really? And if she accepted this part of the truth, did he have the guts to tell her the rest of his suspicions about the night her husband died?

"You got something to say?" she prodded.

"Might as well say it now, since your ten minutes is nearly up."

He took a deep breath, leveled his gaze with hers and blurted it out before he could stop himself again. "I think your husband was assassinated by an American contractor."

Chapter Two

Evan waited for her reaction, ready to duck if her twitching fingers lifted the shotgun. But he saw curiosity in her eyes rather than anger, the first non-hostile expression he'd seen from her since she'd come outside the house.

"MacLear," she murmured, catching him off guard. When he didn't speak immediately, her gaze pierced him like an arrow. "That's who you're talking about, right? MacLear Security's Special Services Unit."

"Yes," he said, stunned. "You knew this already?"

She shook her head slowly. "I don't know it *now*. Why would MacLear target Vince? He never had anything to do with them, even in Kaziristan."

Evan wasn't so sure about that, but he knew better than to voice his nagging suspicions, especially now that he had her actually talking to him. "But MacLear was there."

"And the Special Services Unit was doing special wet-work jobs for Barton Reid for years," she added faintly.

"Allegedly." Anger darkened his voice. Proving Reid's role in the mess had turned out to be harder than expected.

"Allegedly," Megan echoed, her voice tinged with disgust. "Do you think Barton Reid ordered my husband's murder?"

He couldn't tell whether she thought the idea had merit or not, but at least she didn't dismiss the thought outright.

"I think *someone* did. Maybe Reid, and if I can prove it, maybe some of the charges against him will finally stick."

Her tone was bleak. "Good luck with that."

"He's going to walk if we can't tie him to something concrete. You know that. He won't have to pay anything for the terror he put your cousin's family through. Or the hit he put out on your sister-in-law back in March."

Her head cocked and her eyes narrowed. "You know a lot about me and my family."

"I made it my business." He squared his shoulders and met her gaze directly. "I guess my ten minutes are up now. Do I stay or go?"

She was silent a moment before finally giving a single backward jerk of her head and turning toward the house.

As she started up the steps, he let himself into the yard and closed the gate behind him, pausing a moment to let Patton greet him properly. He looked up to find Megan watching him from the open doorway. She'd tucked the phone in the pocket of her running shorts, but the shotgun remained in her hand.

In an instant, he felt a tug low in his belly, an attraction to this backwoods avenging angel, with her fiery hair, stormy eyes and death at her fingertips.

She was dangerous on an entirely different level.

BASED ON THE GRUMBLINGS IN HER husband's letters, Megan had reduced Evan Pike to such a wizened, rule-worshipping paper-rustler in her mind that she'd never stopped to wonder what he really looked like. He was taller than she'd expected, bigger altogether—over six feet tall, a good eight inches taller than Megan herself. His broad, muscular shoulders, flat belly and trim hips would not have been out of place in any army unit, although he'd never been a soldier, according to Vince.

She realized he was aware of her scrutiny when a smile flirted with the corners of his mouth. "Do I pass muster?"

"Remains to be seen." Biting back her annoyance, she carried the shotgun to her bedroom and set it against the cabinet that stood by her door. She never locked it up while she was home, unless one of her cousins brought their kids over for a visit. Gossamer Ridge wasn't exactly a dangerous place, but the Cooper family's run-ins with some very bad actors over the past few years had put her on alert.

She returned to the living room, where Evan stood patiently near the door, waiting for direction. Patton sat on the floor at his feet, gazing at him with a ridiculous look that could only be a doggy grin.

"Nice place," Evan commented.

She looked around the bungalow, his words driving home just how indifferent she'd become to her surroundings. The bungalow was supposed to have been a placeholder until Vince returned from his last tour of duty and took his honorable discharge. They'd already saved up a down payment for a nice piece of land not far from where her cousins' family lived on Gossamer Lake; Vince had planned to do most of the construction of the house himself once they picked out a set of blueprints to work from.

Now the bungalow was purgatory, a lingering place, until she figured out what to do with the years stretching in front of her with no clear purpose.

"Thank you," she responded, wondering if he was merely being polite or if he actually saw something of interest in the drab, utilitarian living room. At least it was clean. She wasn't messy by nature, but Patton couldn't say the same. Between the hair shedding and his habit of shredding his toys until their innards lay scattered about the room like clumps of dirty snow, Patton had proved a high-maintenance companion.

"If you're not comfortable with my being here, Mrs. Randall, we could go elsewhere. Maybe a late breakfast in town?" he suggested.

"I'm not uncomfortable," she denied, the lie obvious even to her own ears. She gestured toward the kitchen doorway. "If you're hungry, though, I have eggs in the fridge. Ham, too." Apparently she was helpless against her habitual hospitality, ingrained by years of living in a Southern small town.

"You don't have to feed me—"

She'd already made the invitation. She didn't intend to jerk it back. "Patton and I haven't eaten yet, either. You're welcome to join us."

She saw his lips quirk. "Gotta love the South. Everybody tries to feed you, even if they hate your guts."

She didn't comment—what could she say, that she didn't hate him? That remained to be seen, didn't it?

She waved at the small breakfast bar near the stove, hiding her amusement when he tried to settle his big frame on one of the small stools. He looked like a giant in a child's chair.

Patton trotted up beside him and sat again, his attention fixed on the newcomer. Evan Pike reached down and scratched the dog's ears as if they were old friends.

"You and Patton knew each other back in Kaziristan?" She washed her hands at the sink.

"I'm the one who found him. Aren't I, boy?" Evan smiled at the dog, who gazed at him as if he were a long-lost friend.

"Vince said he just wandered up one day."

He glanced up at her as if trying to gauge whether she was calling him a liar. She wasn't, really—Vince had been vague about Patton's origins. "He was tiny—barely weaned. He'd crawled under one of the trucks for warmth and probably would've been squashed if I hadn't spotted him as the truck was about to roll out."

She stifled a shudder. Life without Patton around these past four years would've been hell. "Why didn't you send him home to your own wife?"

"I don't have a wife," he answered. "Vince said you loved dogs, so it seemed the right answer."

She dried her hands. "I'm glad to have him."

"He looks great. Much more polite than he was back at the base." His smile crinkled the skin around his eyes and made his whole face come alive. The skin on her back rippled at the sight, sparking a flutter of alarm.

Was she attracted to him? Good grief, what terrible timing for that slumbering part of herself to stagger back to life. She'd already decided that, short of being married to Vince Randall for life, being his widow was the only other option. If she couldn't have Vince back, she'd rather be alone.

Attraction or no attraction.

She ignored the tug in her gut and crossed to the refrigerator to pull a couple of brown-shelled eggs from the bin. "Scrambled or fried?"

"Whichever's easier," he answered. "May I use the sink to wash my hands?"

"Of course," she answered, though she immediately regretted not sending him down the hall to the bathroom instead. Partitioned from the breakfast nook by the counter bar, this section of the kitchen was small, and his broad-shouldered presence seemed to reduce the size by half.

Their arms brushed as she reached past him for the frying pan. She gritted her teeth against the heat flooding her body.

Her sisters had been urging her to dip her toe in the dating pool again. She'd always ignored the suggestion, certain she was the kind of woman who mated for life. She'd had her one great love. She didn't need a pale imitation.

Still, if she'd had a steady boyfriend now, she doubted she'd be standing here, crowded by a big, inconveniently attractive man and feeling like a virginal sixteen-year-old at her first high school dance.

He dried his hands on a paper towel and looked down at her, making her feel small and vulnerable. She didn't like the sensation. "Garbage can?"

She held out her hand. "It's under the bar—I'll throw it away for you. Go. Sit." *And get your enor-*

mous male self out of my kitchen before I do something embarrassing.

"Sure I can't help with something?"

Why not? It would keep him occupied and out of her way. "There's bread in that box." She waved at the toaster next to him on the bar. "Think you can handle toast?"

"Sure."

She plated the eggs, saving a little for Patton's bowl, and carried the plates over to the bar. He added slices of toast.

Rather than sitting on the stool beside Evan, she stood across from him at the bar to eat.

"Good," he commented after a bite. "Thanks."

"You're welcome."

The silence between them thickened. Halfway through her eggs and toast, Megan could stand it no more. "What makes you think MacLear had anything to do with Vince's death? Didn't the army investigate? Are you saying they covered it up?"

"The official story about your husband's death in the line of duty doesn't match up to the evidence," Evan answered flatly. "There are big holes in the story, questions nobody can—or will—answer. Believe me, I've tried to get those answers, but it didn't take long to hit a wall. But I don't think the army investigators are the ones covering things up."

"Are you here in an official Pentagon capacity?"

He shook his head. "I don't work at the Pentagon anymore."

That caught her by surprise. "Vince said you were practically married to the place."

"We got a divorce." That smile came out to play again, this time tinged with regret. "Irreconcilable differences."

No longer hungry, she scraped the rest of her eggs into Patton's bowl, giving the dog a quick scratch behind the ears. "Were you fired?" she asked.

"I would've been if I hadn't resigned."

"Because you're asking questions about Vince's death?"

"Yes."

"None of Vince's buddies ever suggested it was anything but a rebel attack. Don't you think someone would have said something to me if there were questions?"

"They may not have known there were questions."

She shook her head, still not able to make sense of what he was trying to tell her. "Vince died four years ago. If you had questions, why'd it take so long to ask them?"

His gaze lifted reluctantly. "I didn't want to have questions. I didn't want to make waves."

She didn't know whether to feel sorry for him or angry at him. "How long did you sit on your suspicions?"

"Not the whole time. I had—" He paused, as if searching for the right words. "I had a wild thought, at the time it happened. Because of how it happened. We were protecting civilians against al Adar at the time—"

"You mean Vince and his men were protecting them from al Adar," she corrected, more fiercely than she'd intended.

He looked chastened. "Right. And al Adar isn't known for sniper hits. They're more the 'plant a sneaky bomb' types."

"So you wondered why they'd chosen to kill a soldier sniper-style?"

"That, and I wondered how they'd managed it. I asked around at the time—nobody had ever heard of al Adar snipers."

"There's always a first time," she said, though she was beginning to understand why Evan Pike might've had questions.

"Nobody makes that kind of shot the first time," Evan disagreed. "One clean round, straight through the heart, no chance of survival?"

"Maybe the shooter was so close it wasn't a tough shot."

Evan shook his head. "Your husband's patrol team searched immediately for the shooter. He was nowhere close enough to make an easy shot. And nothing we know about the rebels in Kaziristan suggests they have the training or weapons necessary to pull off that sort of sharpshooting."

"Okay," she conceded. "Maybe it wasn't al Adar. But what makes you think MacLear's Special Services Unit was behind it? It could have been rogue elements of the Kaziri army. Some of them still carry Dragunovs—"

He looked surprised by her knowledge. "Not a Dragunov. Wrong caliber. The round that killed your husband was a 7.62 x 51mm NATO round. Dragunovs shoot the old 7.62 Russians."

"So the Kaziris got their hands on some NATO rifles," she countered. "God knows there's probably a ton of surplus lying around in Central Asia after the past few years—"

Evan shook his head. "Still doesn't explain the shot accuracy. I checked with CIA and military intelligence. Nobody in the Kaziri army is thought to be any good with precision rifles. Same with al Adar. Whoever shot your husband knew what he was doing, and right now, none of the Kaziris fall under that category."

Megan frowned, unease prickling in her belly. "Okay. Let's say, for the sake of argument, that you're right. It wasn't al Adar and it wasn't anyone in the Kaziri army. Could it have been friendly fire?"

"All units in the area were accounted for at the time of the shooting," he answered. "No live fire going on anywhere within thirty klicks—kilometers—of the checkpoint where your husband was shot."

"I know what a klick is."

"Sorry. Didn't want to presume."

She hated to ask the question, but it couldn't be ignored. "Could it have been one of Vince's men?"

"Not unless they were all in on it," Evan replied. He pushed aside his half-eaten plate of eggs and leaned toward her. "How well did you know the men in his unit?"

"Moderately well," she answered. "We didn't live in base housing, but we socialized some. I haven't seen any of them in a while, though. Not since the unit returned stateside. I went to welcome them back."

"Yeah? Their instigation or yours?"

"Mine," she admitted. "I drove over to Fort Benning to join the families waiting to greet them. I just needed to talk to the last people to see Vince."

"How was the meeting?" He sounded curious.

She tried to replay the meeting in her head, to catch all the details, all the nuances. "I talked to Rafe Delgado first." Delgado had been impossibly young, she remembered. Barely in his twenties, his black hair shorn to a glossy flat top, his fatigues soiled and rumpled from the long trip home. He'd smelled of sweat and grime and hard work, and she remembered thinking how eagerly she'd have buried herself in the smell and the dirt if Vince had been the one standing in front of her. "His mother was there to greet him, but he gave me a few minutes. Thanked me for coming, said Vince would have appreciated it."

"Anything else?"

Megan shook her head. "I didn't want to make anyone feel uncomfortable. I probably shouldn't have gone there in the first place, but I felt—" The words caught in her throat, and she blinked back the moisture in her stinging eyes. "Vince would have wanted me to see them home."

Evan nodded. "The shot didn't come from close quarters. None of his men shot him, although I can't be sure that none of them set him up."

"You can't be sure of anything, can you?" She straightened her shoulders. "Maybe you think this is some sort of penance you have to pay for helping enforce the rules that Vince believed put his men in danger. But you didn't shoot him. You didn't even make the rules that put him in danger. I don't really blame you. You just did your job."

"I know that," he said, his voice sharp for the first time. His lips pressed into a tight line and his voice softened when he spoke again. "I'm not going to lie—I do feel guilty. I knew some of the restrictions we were putting on our soldiers made life harder for them. It made their jobs more dangerous. But we were trying to save a country from falling to a violent and dangerous group of terrorists. The last thing we needed—"

"Was to alienate the people you were trying to

protect," she finished for him, trying not to sound bitter. "I know."

"It was the better of two bad choices," he said quietly. "I can wrap my head around it intellectually, but I can't get the sight of your husband out of my head."

She arched an eyebrow. "You saw Vince after he died?"

"I was at the base when they brought his body back," he murmured. "His buddies weren't happy to see me."

She supposed not. "So you think you need to make it up to Vince and the other men. But why come tell me things you can't even prove are true? What do you want from me?"

"I know Vince wrote letters home. A lot of them. It's almost all he did on his downtime—write letters home. I'm betting most of them were to you."

She bit back a new rush of emotion.

"I need to see those letters."

A flood of outrage ripped through her. "No."

"I realize there were personal things you wouldn't want me to read—"

"It was *all* personal," she snapped. "I'm not letting you see any of them."

"He never wrote about what was going on in Kaziristan?"

Of course he had, but that didn't change anything. "Those letters are all I have left that really feels like him. I don't share them with anyone."

Frustration gleamed in his green eyes. "Will you at least consider rereading the letters to see if there's anything in there that resonates with you based on—" A low trilling noise coming from the vicinity of his jeans pocket interrupted, eliciting an irritated growl from him. He checked the display, frowning at what he saw.

"What is it?" she asked before she could stop herself.

"I think it's the motel." He answered. "Evan Pike."

She watched his expression shift as he listened to the person on the other end of the line, going from curious to alarmed. "What time?" he asked. He paused as he apparently got an answer, then added. "I'll be there in ten minutes. Thank you for calling."

"Is something wrong?" she asked.

He shoved the phone back into his jeans pocket. "Someone broke into my motel room this morning. Housekeeping discovered the mess."

"How did they know it was a break-in?" Megan asked. "I mean, some people are just messy—"

"Apparently a message was written on the dresser mirror," he answered, already moving toward the front of the house. "Thank you for your time, Mrs. Randall. And the food."

Patton jumped up to go to the door with Evan, and Megan followed in their wake, alarm coiling like a snake in her gut. She caught Evan's arm as he reached the door. "What message?"

He looked at her, his expression dark with anger. "It said, 'Go home or she'll regret it.'"

Chapter Three

"Am I the 'she' in question?" Megan's low question broke the thickening silence in the ransacked motel room.

Whoever tossed the place had wanted to leave a clear message. Evan's clothes lay scattered across the room, his toiletries strewn about. An entire tube of toothpaste had been squeezed out into the sink of motel bathroom. Fortunately his briefcase full of notes on Vince Randall's shooting had been with him in the car.

"I think so. I haven't been shy with my questions about your husband's death."

She stared at the block letters painted in white shoe polish on the mirror. "Why haven't I heard about it before?"

"I went through Pentagon channels. It wasn't in their interest to involve you."

"You think someone at the Pentagon broke in and left a message on your mirror?" Her drawling voice dripped skepticism.

"No, but someone in D.C. may have said the wrong thing to the wrong person."

"The 'wrong person' being someone formerly connected with MacLear Security?"

He nodded. "They scattered like roaches after their illegal activities came to light. We don't even know who some of them were—you know that."

Members of her extended family had already clashed with MacLear Security's former Special Services Unit, a small cadre of black ops agents MacLear's CEO, Jackson Melville, had assembled from a pool of talented but corruptible field operatives. The SSU's attempt to kidnap her cousin's son had led to their downfall.

And just two months ago, a group of former SSU agents had tried to carry out a hit on an ex-CIA agent named Amanda Caldwell. Megan's brother Rick had nearly lost his own life helping Amanda turn the tables on her attackers.

"We know a least a few of their names," Megan said. "Cooper Security's been putting together a dossier on the SSU ever since we discovered several had reunited with others in their unit."

"Your brother must know many of them," he said carefully. Rick Cooper had been a MacLear Security agent for over a decade before the company collapsed under the weight of SSU scandal, but as far as Evan knew, Rick's work with MacLear had been completely legit. He had a good reputation among the foreign service agents Evan had spoken with.

"Rick knows some by name," Megan answered carefully. "But not all. I guess you know what happened back in March."

Evan nodded. "What your brother and his friend told Senator Blackledge created one hell of a stir at CIA," he told her. "I hear there's an internal investigation going on there."

Megan didn't look surprised. "Amanda still has contacts at CIA who keep her updated with what they can legally share."

"She's stuck around?" He was surprised. "I'd figured she'd just blended back into the woodwork again." CIA agents generally reminded him a little of cockroaches, too.

"She married Rick," Megan said with a smile. "You should bring them in on this, if you really think the SSU is behind all this." She waved at the mirror. "Or if you want to call the cops, I have family in the local agencies."

He turned to face her. "How would you handle it?"

She appeared surprised he'd consulted her. "I'd call my family," she said. "If this really is connected to the SSU, we Coopers all have a stake in it."

He looked at the mirror. Back home, if he'd walked in to find his apartment trashed and a warning message on his mirror, he'd have called the cops. Gone through regular channels. Let the system work.

It was how he'd handled his initial suspicions about Vince Randall's death, too.

And look how well that had worked out.

He turned back to Megan. "Okay. Call your family."

THOUGH MEGAN WAS USED to being surrounded by large numbers of Coopers at any given time, Evan Pike seemed overwhelmed by the sudden convergence of over a dozen Coopers at the Piedmont Motor Inn. In a virtual convoy of SUVs and pickup trucks, they came down Piedmont Road and swung into the parking lot in front of Evan's room.

"How many Coopers are there?" Evan asked quietly as they piled out of the vehicles.

"Too many to count," she warned. "Coopers believe in going forth and multiplying."

Megan's eldest brother, Jesse, arrived first, but there were over a dozen other Coopers—or Cooper in-laws—right on his heels, including three sheriff's department deputies, a Gossamer Ridge Police detective and seven Cooper Security agents, not counting herself.

As the one with jurisdiction, Kristen Cooper, the police detective, took charge of the scene, handing out assignments. While the rest of the family spread out to talk to other motel visitors and staffers, Jesse, Rick, Rick's wife, Amanda, and Megan joined Evan inside the motel room.

Jesse surveyed the mess, his dark eyes settling

on the mirror. "Why would someone threaten you by threatening Megan? You don't even know each other."

"I'm investigating her husband's death."

Jesse shot Evan a sharp look. "You really think Vince was assassinated?"

"It's more likely than not," Evan replied carefully, sounding every inch the lawyer he was.

Jesse pulled a business card from the pocket of his suit jacket and handed it to Evan. "If you'd like our help, this is where you can contact me. Leave my sister out of it."

Megan whirled on her brother, dismayed. "You don't get to make that decision, Jesse."

"You want to go through this?" he asked, meeting her anger without flinching. "Really?"

"If there's a chance Vince was murdered, I want to be part of the investigation."

Her brother closed his big hand over her shoulder. "Meggie, please. You're too close to this to be objective, and no good can come from going back to those days again. You're in a better state now—"

She stared at him, stunned. A better state? "You make it sound like I took to my bed after Vince died."

Jesse glanced at Evan. "If I need to make it an order—"

Fire leapt in her gut. "You're not my parent and if you think you'll get anywhere throwing your weight around as my boss, forget it. I'll quit Cooper Security in a heartbeat."

Jesse's lips thinned to a line. "Fine. If you want in, you're in—"

"I haven't brought any of you in on the investigation," Evan spoke up.

Megan whipped around to face him, trying to calm the anger roiling in her belly. "If you're right about any of this—about the SSU's involvement, about a high-level government cover-up—you're going to need all the help you can get."

"We have a stake in bringing down the SSU," Rick spoke up from the corner of the room. "We have a company full of trained, skilled analysts and field operatives at your disposal."

"For how big a fee?" Evan's tone was wary.

"For free," Megan spoke up, shooting her brothers a look daring them to disagree.

"I can't have a big crew of people getting in the middle of this investigation," Evan warned. "We have to fly under the radar as much as possible."

"Clearly, you're already on somebody's radar." Amanda gestured toward the mirror.

"And having half of Chickasaw County descending on this motel probably isn't helping," Evan added grimly.

"Or maybe it'll be a warning to the people who did this," Megan countered. "People have your back."

"I'm not sure they'll see that as a flaw in their

plan," Rick murmured. "You can't tell me there aren't some SSU guys out there still angry about how things went down back in March up on the mountain."

"I heard about that," Evan said. "You were lucky to live through that siege. You were outnumbered, what—three to one?"

"I know we were lucky," Rick said. "But I agree— low profile's the way to go for now. If there's a cover- up going on, keeping it simple will make it harder for them to predict your moves. If they know your plans ahead of time, they'll have all their messes cleaned up long before you get there."

"Okay, we take this deep cover, then," Jesse said. "I can have someone put out a story that teenage vandals hit the motel and left a mess in one of the rooms. You'll need to move out of here, though."

"Cooper Cove Properties has some cabins for rent. They could put you up at off-season rates," Megan suggested. "It's five minutes from my house, fifteen from our office in Maybridge, and you'll be surrounded by Coopers with guns."

Evan's lips curved. "Not sure that's reassuring."

"You should register under a fake name," Megan suggested.

A knock on the door interrupted. Megan opened the door to Kristen, her cousin Sam's wife and the Gossamer Ridge police detective heading the case. The slim blonde edged past Megan and took a look at the message on the mirror again. "Not much subtlety with this bunch."

"I doubt you'll find anything useful," Evan warned as she pulled out an evidence-gathering kit. "They had over an hour to toss the place. These people know how to get rid of evidence."

"You're probably right, but I don't mind taking a look around if you're okay with that."

He held up his hands. "Knock yourself out."

EVAN'S PREDICTION PANNED OUT. Except for the mess they'd strewn in their wake, whoever had searched his room hadn't left any evidence of their own behind.

The motel was only partially occupied, though it was the start of tourist season, and many of those guests appeared to be out for the day already, no doubt enjoying the warm May sunshine and good fishing on the lake. Evan had purposefully asked for a room as far from other guests as possible, so even the people still in their rooms that morning hadn't been close enough to notice anything useful. Nor had the motel manager noticed anything out of the ordinary, and the extra key to Evan's room was in the locked drawer where the staff kept the spares.

Not that an SSU agent would have needed a key.

The more intriguing part of his time spent surrounded by various and sundry Coopers was watching how they treated Megan Randall. Love and affection was evident in abundance, but beneath it all lurked an unexpected sense that they saw her as a fragile flower to be handled with gentleness and delicacy.

The idea that Megan Randall was easily breakable conflicted with his own experience. On the contrary, the woman had a spine of steel and a soul of fire. Get too close, he was certain, and she could burn a man alive with her intensity.

Clearly, she'd loved her husband. She must have mourned him deeply. But how bad had it been for her, that her family would so clearly fear a relapse after all this time?

Jesse Cooper had said she was in a better state. Better than what?

Was she hiding a vulnerability he couldn't see? If he shared his suspicion that Vince Randall may have been working with the SSU in Kaziristan— that his death had been payback for backing out of a deal—would she fall apart completely?

He had a lot to think about, going forward, especially if Megan Randall was going to take part in his investigation.

Around noon, one of Megan's cousins, Hannah Patterson, rode with him up the rise to a sprawling bungalow about halfway up the mountain, with a glancing view over the top of the tree line of the lake below. It would be his residence the rest of his time in Chickasaw County.

"I've turned on the power and water, and you're

free to enjoy any of the amenities," Hannah said as she handed over the key. "I mean, don't leave all the appliances and lights running all day or anything, but feel free to fill up the Jacuzzi and have a soak."

"Do you have a map of your properties?" he asked, tucking the key in his jeans pocket.

She nodded. "Good idea—if you're trying to keep a low profile, it's probably good to know the lay of the land. I'll get one for you. Oh, before I forget—my brother Gabe put some fish fillets in the freezer for you—bluegill and catfish, mostly. I hope you like fish."

"Thank you. Very generous. You want a ride back down the mountain?"

She shook her head. "It's not far, and I'm going to stop by to check on some other guests down the mountain, make sure they have everything they need. Which reminds me—Megan said to tell you she's doing some grocery shopping for you, so you should be set for a few days." She handed him a card. "My cell number's on there. Any problems, give me a call and I can have a dozen armed and dangerous Coopers up here in minutes." She started down the porch steps.

"That happen a lot?" he called after her.

She turned, flashing him a wry grin. "Didn't used to. But we've seen our share of troubles the past few years." She headed down the mountain on foot, disappearing into the thick woods beyond the clearing where his cabin sat.

He let himself inside, taking in the rustic wood décor. It was definitely a cabin, but the furniture looked large and comfortable, and the television in the front room was enormous and appeared to come with satellite hook-up.

Exploring further, he found the hot tub she mentioned, along with a surprisingly roomy kitchen area with new appliances and a sunny breakfast nook next to a window overlooking the wooded rise of the mountain behind the cabin.

Definitely better than the motel room, he thought.

Resisting the siren call of the hot tub, he unpacked his things from the car and took them inside. Rick Cooper had checked the motel room and all his belongings for listening or GPS devices before they'd let him take any of his things with him, so at least he didn't have to worry about someone tracking him down any time soon.

But the show of Coopers at the motel still had him worried. How hard would it be to connect the Coopers to the Cooper Cove rental properties? Surely they'd think to look here at the cabins for him, sooner or later.

And then what? Kill him for his notes?

He had copies of everything, stashed in a safe place that wouldn't easily be tracked to him. He even had left instructions with his lawyer on what to do if something happened to him. Paranoid, perhaps, but if the last four years had taught him any-thing, it was that even if you kept your head down and tried to stay out of trouble, trouble still had a nasty way of finding you.

This time, however, he planned to be prepared.

"WHAT DO WE REALLY KNOW about this guy?"

On the other end of the cell phone line, Megan's sister Shannon sounded more miffed than worried, probably because Jesse, Isabel and the rest of the Coopers had left her out of the trip to Evan's motel room.

"We don't know much," Megan admitted. "Vince mentioned his name in some of his letters home."

"Is someone going to run a background check? I could help with that."

Megan smiled as she tucked the phone under her chin and reached up to pull a can of chili from the grocery store shelf. Though she was an employee of the security agency along with the rest of them, computer tech and archivist Shannon never got any time in the field. She'd recently become vocal about wanting to do more field investigative work and had gone so far as to line up several Informa-tion Technology grads for interviews with Jesse recently without consulting him first.

He hadn't been amused. Maybe leaving Shannon out had been his way of driving home his authority at the agency. Megan personally thought her baby sister should get the chance to prove herself in the field, just as the rest of them had.

"Call Jesse and offer your help," Megan suggested.

"Yeah, that'll go over well," Shannon grumbled. "Where are you, anyway?"

"Piggly Wiggly in Maybridge, picking up supplies for our visitor," she answered, grabbing more cans of soup from the shelves. "We all agreed he shouldn't be out and about much. Someone could be targeting him."

The hair at the back of her neck prickled, and she turned her head to check behind her. Down the aisle, about twenty feet away, stood a man in black jeans and a dark green long-sleeved T-shirt. The sleeves were rolled up to his elbows, and when he reached up to pull something from the shelf, she could see a tribal symbol tattoo on the inside of his right arm.

He never looked at her, but she had the sense he was acutely aware of her presence.

"Sure, Jesse lets you play babysitter with some stranger in danger, but I don't even get to help with a background check."

"Shannon, I'm on your side. You know I am." Megan moved quickly around the corner, skipping the next two aisles and heading down the third one, her nerves still jangling. "But if you don't stop whining about being left out, that could change."

"I know I sound like a broken record, but I'm

twenty-six years old. Jesse was a lot younger than that when he went overseas armed with a big gun to face down a whole world full of people who wanted him dead because he was an American. Maybe I should've joined the marines and then he'd take me seriously."

"Maybe if you didn't sound like a bored teenager when you asked him to let you do things—"

Shannon made a growling noise of frustration. "Okay. I'll work on that. And I think I will offer to help with the background check. It's mostly desk work. He can't get all crazy about me doing that, right?"

"That's the spirit." Megan dropped a box of crackers into her buggy and slanted a quick look over her shoulder. The man with the tattoo was at the other end of the aisle, gazing at the products on the shelves in front of him.

Was it a coincidence he'd skipped the same aisles she had?

She turned the corner again and backtracked, moving down the previous aisle. She walked at a leisurely pace, pretending to study the products, though she saw none of them, her attention focused on the sound of footsteps behind her. She reached the end of the aisle, turned and glanced back at the aisle she was leaving.

Tattoo man was halfway down the aisle, gazing with earnest interest at an array of spices.

Megan was nowhere near finished with the shopping she'd planned, but she detoured straight to the checkout counter and paid for her selections. She saw no sign of the tattooed man while she was paying the bill, nor did she spot him outside in the parking lot when she loaded the groceries into her Jeep Wrangler and drove east toward Gossamer Ridge.

She didn't spot anyone following her, but just in case, she went home instead of heading up the mountain to the cabin where Evan Pike was staying. Parking out front, she carried the bag of groceries inside in case anyone was watching.

A blast of refrigerated air washed over her when she let herself in. She braced herself for Patton's exuberant hello, listening for the clatter of his claws on her scuffed-up hardwood floors.

But there was only silence.

"Patton?" Megan stepped farther into the house, her heart pounding. The silence was almost tangible, like a hand squeezing her throat until she couldn't breathe.

She set down the bag quietly and detoured into the bedroom to retrieve her Ruger. But before she reached the bedside table where she kept it, she found Patton lying on the floor beside her bed.

Unmoving.

Chapter Four

The Gossamer Ridge Pet Clinic seemed to blend into the side of the mountain, hewn of the same russet stone that made up the prominent rock faces that had been visible on the drive down the mountain. Rick Cooper parked next to a blue Jeep in the parking lot, got out and hurried up the walk, leaving Evan to catch up.

Rick had surprised him a few minutes ago with news of the break-in at Megan's house. The dog, he said, was alive but unresponsive. Megan had sent him to pick up Evan. "Said you'd want to be there," Rick had told him tersely on the way out.

Inside the vet clinic, Evan spotted Megan at the front counter, talking to the woman behind the desk. She turned at the sound of the door opening, relief evident in her gray eyes. "Patton's going to be okay. Whoever broke in shot him with a tranquilizer dart, but he's already coming around."

Evan released a pent-up breath. "What about your place? Did they take anything?"

"I didn't stop to check," she admitted. "I was

afraid if I didn't get him right to the vet…" She raked her fingers through her hair. "They want to keep him overnight to make sure he doesn't have any ill effects from the tranquilizer, so I guess I might as well go home now and see what the damage is."

She seemed angry but not sick with worry, which meant she hadn't yet realized just what she might find missing when she finally made it back home.

But Evan had. If they'd bothered to tranquilize the dog, this break-in was more than a warning. They'd been looking for something in particular and needed time to find it.

He had a sick feeling he knew exactly what it was.

Within a minute of arriving at Megan's house, his fear was confirmed. Megan emerged from her room, fire dancing in her eyes. "The only thing missing is a box of letters from Vince."

"I'm so sorry," Evan said, heartsick. Beyond the setback to his investigation, losing those letters had to be like losing part of her husband all over again.

She frowned. "You knew what they came for, didn't you?"

"I suspected," he admitted. "Once Rick told me the place had been tossed. They want the evidence I'm looking for. I'm sorry about those letters—"

To his surprise, she started to laugh. "Talk about working in mysterious ways."

"What?"

Her laughter faded to a smile. "When you showed up this morning, wanting to see the letters, it put me on guard. I wasn't sure you wouldn't try to steal them yourself—"

"You don't think I had anything to do—"

"No," she said quickly. "I don't. But I decided to put his letters in a safe place. Before I went grocery shopping, I ran the letters over to Cooper Security and put them in one of our safes." Her grin was downright smug.

"But you said they took his letters—"

"Teenage stuff. I'll miss them, but they're not the same as the letters he wrote after we married and he went off to war." Her smile faded. "So I guess I should thank you."

"For being so untrustworthy you hid your letters from me?"

"Yes." Her smile flitted back to life, stoking the slow burn in his gut that seemed to flicker to life whenever she flashed her pretty teeth at him. He'd never considered wiry redheads his type, but his body seemed to have other ideas.

"We should get you back to the cabin before people start noticing the stranger in our midst," she said quietly, glancing toward the uniformed officers guarding the front of her house while detectives continued gathering evidence inside.

"You're not kin to them, too?" He nodded toward the uniformed officers, his voice equally hushed.

She cut her eyes at him. "Very funny. I know them by name but not well enough to trust them with my secrets."

"You think we could be dealing with inside in-filtrators?"

"Money opens doors." She glanced at the police officers again. "Some folks around here barely make ends meet. If you're right about the SSU being behind Vince's death, somebody paid them well to do it."

"Barton Reid?" Evan knew the former State Department official had been working out of the U.S. Embassy in Kaziristan at the time of Vince Randall's death. MacLear also had agents in the country then, which was why MacLear's secret operatives were his prime suspects in Randall's death.

That, and the fact that some of Vince Randall's men had mentioned the sergeant had been spending a lot of time by himself in Tablis over the last couple of weeks before his death. More than usual.

More than necessary.

"Reid was trying to build himself a power base outside the law," he added. "Maybe now he's trying to cover his tracks to avoid jail time and even get back some of his power."

"No way the State Department takes him back. They can't look past the scandal, even if the case never goes to trial."

"I wasn't thinking about power at State." Evan flattened his hand against the middle of her back, nudging her toward the empty kitchen. The second his fingers touched the skin-heated cotton of her T-shirt, he felt a jolt of desire as powerful as a kick in the gut. He looked down and found Megan gazing up at him with wide gray eyes, her cheeks pink and her lips parted.

She was standing close enough to kiss, and damned if he didn't want to do it.

He dropped his hand from her back and stepped away. But putting distance between them didn't quell his simmering desire.

He cleared his throat, keeping his voice low. "Barton Reid may be rebuilding the SSU as his own personal army, without the veneer of MacLear to give them the air of legitimacy."

"We think the SSU are freelancers." Megan moved toward him, her voice as quiet as his own. "We know Khalid Mazir hired some of them to kill my sister-in-law Amanda so she couldn't connect Mazir to al Adar."

Evan nodded. Khalid Mazir, the son of a beloved Kaziri democratic reformer, Zoli Mazir, had chosen violence and power over his father's love for law and compromise. Khalid had nearly deceived the peace-hungry citizens of Kaziristan into making him president before Amanda Cooper had identified him as the terrorist who'd abducted and tortured her while she was working for the CIA.

"But who told Mazir about the SSU?" he asked.

"How would he know they were still out there, willing to kill for money?"

Megan's eyes narrowed. "He must have heard it from the man who once owned the SSU, lock, stock and barrel. Barton Reid."

Evan nodded. "He knew the Mazirs well. Including Khalid."

Megan tilted her chin toward him, giving him a tantalizing view of her soft, full lips. "Reid wanted Khalid Mazir in power, which means he almost certainly had something on him, something he thought he could use to control him."

"Maybe just knowing he was a terrorist was enough." Evan dragged his gaze from her lips and spotted one of the police officers passing close to the doorway to the kitchen. "They'll be looking around awhile longer. Want to get out of here?"

She followed his gaze as the police officer settled close enough to the kitchen that he would surely overhear anything they said above a whisper. Her brow furrowed. "I'll tell Kristen we're leaving."

Evan took a deep, bracing breath as she walked away, willing his body back under control. The way her well-toned legs flexed beneath the tight denim of her jeans didn't help.

She returned with a backpack slung over one shoulder and a large black Ruger clipped to her waistband. As he eyed the weapon, she motioned for him to follow her out the back door.

"Where are we going?" he asked as she bypassed the driveway and headed into the woods butting up to the back of the house.

Over her shoulder, she flashed him a mysterious smile.

MEGAN LED EVAN PIKE halfway up the southern face of Gossamer Mountain. To his credit, he kept pace without any sign of struggle. Maybe he'd come by those lean muscles honestly after all.

Where she was taking him, they could at least speak with some semblance of privacy. While she didn't think Jimmy Long had been trying to eavesdrop, she knew the young cop and his wife were struggling to make ends meet, with a baby on the way. If someone offered him a grand to tell what he overheard at Megan's house, could he resist the much-needed money?

"It's a valid worry," Evan agreed when she shared her thoughts with him a few minutes later as they paused atop a rise. "Money talks—the military's known that for years."

"A man will do things he wouldn't normally do if it means he can take care of his family." She pulled two bottles of water from her backpack and handed one to Evan.

Evan eyed the backpack. "You should have let me carry that part of the way—"

"You can carry it back when we're really tired." She grinned and took a couple of swigs of water, gesturing toward the downhill path. "Come on, we're almost there."

The sounds of the creek burbled through the dense woods, guiding the way down the twisting footpath. They hiked around a stone outcropping and the creek came into view, snaking through the woods like a shiny brown serpent.

"Missacoula Creek," she said aloud, descending to the water's edge, where several flat boulders formed a natural bench along the bank. She sat on one, discarding shoes and socks to dip her feet in the cool waters of the creek. She sighed with pleasure.

"Not much chance of being overheard here." Evan sat beside her, his gaze dropping to her bare feet. "You come here often?"

"Not often enough," she said with a sigh. "Down a hundred yards that way, the creek widens out to create a deep hole. The water's so clear you can swim with your eyes open and see little bluegills and pumpkinseeds swimming around you." Just the thought of it made her happy, a sweet reminder of days spent there with her brothers and sisters.

"Sounds like fun."

"My dad used to bring us out here in the summer when we were younger. He was a cop, and he didn't have a lot of days off to play with us, so he always tried to make it special, especially after Mom left."

"I'm sorry." At the questioning look she shot him, he added, "About your mother."

"It was a long time ago. And it's not like we never see her. She drops back in every year or so to see how we're doing." Megan knew her brothers and sisters found it harder to forgive her mother than she did, but she'd figured out a long time ago that their parents were still in love. They'd never divorced, despite Jean Cooper staying away from Chickasaw County sometimes for a year at a time, because neither wanted to be with anyone else. Even if they couldn't live happily together.

"My parents weren't even speaking by the end of their marriage." A bleak tone threaded through his low voice.

"I'm sorry."

"It was always a difficult marriage, but it fell apart completely after my brother's death," Evan said quietly. "He was a relief worker. A drug cartel kidnapped him, and the charity he worked with couldn't ransom him. So they killed him instead." The haggard look on his face suggested it hadn't been an easy death.

Megan supposed it wouldn't have been. She'd heard stories about drug cartels before—one had hounded her cousin Luke and his family for years. "It wasn't the Cordero gang from Sanselmo, was it?"

He shook his head. "At least I'd know they were dead or captured now." He managed a grim smile. "Justice served, thanks to your cousins, I hear."

"My brother Rick was in on that raid, too," she

said, remembering that tense time almost a year ago when a South American drug lord had kidnapped her cousin's son. "He helped hunt them down and get Mike back."

"You Coopers seem like good people to have at your back in a battle." Evan sounded thoughtful. "I may need some of that help before this is over with."

"What do you want to accomplish? Proving Vince's death was murder? You still don't know who did it."

"If we tie his death to Barton Reid, we bolster the case against him. So he doesn't get away with what he's done."

"That's a big if."

"Someone broke into your house. Someone broke into my motel room. That's not a coincidence."

She couldn't argue, especially when she thought about the man at the grocery store— "Oh!" She looked up at him. "I forgot to tell you." She described the tattooed man who had seemed to trail her around the store. "I don't think he followed me home, though. And he certainly couldn't have been trashing my house. So maybe I just imagined it."

"What kind of tattoo was it?" Evan asked.

"Something tribal. All black and kind of spiky." Her experience with tattoos was limited to Vince's crossed rifles tattoo above his left shoulder blade, and the Marine Corps emblems her brothers Jesse and Wade wore on their left arms.

Evan picked up a nearby twig and traced an image in the dirt at his feet. A crude but recognizable shape took form—a spider, with eight long, spiky legs and two short, sharp pincers. "Did it look like this?"

"That's it," she said, her gut coiling in a knot. How could he have known? Unless—

She dropped her hand to the Ruger on her hip.

Evan's gaze followed the movement of her hand. "I'm not armed," he said, his voice tense.

"How did you know what the tattoo looked like?"

"I've seen it before. Two years ago, Cordero's men killed an SSU operative, Thomas Phelan." Evan gave her a pointed look. "You may know Thomas Phelan as Tristan Peterson."

Megan nodded. "He was one of the MacLear operatives who snatched my cousin's little boy."

"He had a tattoo like that just above his left shoulder blade. I've also seen photos of the same tattoo pattern on the former SSU operatives arrested in March when they went after your brother and his wife."

A snapping sound caught Megan's ear. As she listened for a repeat, she realized the woods around them had fallen unusually quiet, as if the animals and birds had all stopped moving. She and Evan had been sitting here long enough that the woodland animals should have already resumed their usual routines.

Was someone out there, just out of sight?

She casually turned her face toward the noise and listened.

There. Another soft cracking sound.

She looked at Evan. "Just a squirrel, I guess."

She pulled her shoes and socks on unhurriedly, then reached across and caught Evan's hand in hers.

His gaze snapped up to meet hers.

"There's someone out there," she said so quietly that he bent forward to hear her. Her heart quickened as the heat of his body surrounded her. Up close, she got a good look at the flecks of gold suddenly obvious in his warm green eyes. It took a second to regain her wits.

"What do you want to do?" he asked, his voice as soft as her own. He leaned closer, as if to whisper intimately in her ear. His cheek brushed hers and a shock of raw physical need bolted through her like a mustang freed from its tether.

Her breath hitching, she struggled not to turn her face to his, to feel skin on skin again, just for a moment. To remember what it felt like to be touched by a man, even if that man wasn't Vince Randall.

But the prickling sensation on her back proved more urgent. "Right now, we're sitting ducks for whoever's out there. I don't care for that feeling."

"I don't, either," he murmured.

She tightened her grip on his hand, finding it

warm and slightly rough, as if he did more with his hands than light office work. With a tug, she drew him off the river boulders and down to the sandy bank below, putting the rocks between them and whoever was out there in the woods.

"Now what?" he asked.

She pulled the Ruger out of her hip holster and checked the clip. "I know you said you weren't armed—"

"I have this." He pulled a multi-blade knife from his pocket. "And this," he added, meeting her gaze with a look of apology as he produced a Kel-Tec P32 pistol from an ankle holster hidden beneath the right leg of his jeans.

"We'll talk about the lie later," she murmured.

"Are you sure it's not someone in your family?"

"We'd never have heard them," she answered with confidence. "My dad taught us how to get around the woods in silence when we were just kids. He was the best I've ever seen at it."

"Did you actually see anyone?"

"No. But I felt him."

Evan studied her through narrowed eyes as if considering whether to trust her judgment. Finally, he nodded. "If someone's sneaking around, it's to eavesdrop or to ambush."

"Which is it?" she asked.

"Eavesdrop," he answered after a brief hesitation. "By now, whoever took your stuff has had time to realize what he's looking for isn't there. He needs to find out where it is."

She looked up to find his gaze on her lips. His intentions remained murky, for he held himself as far away from her as their close proximity would allow. But the desire in his green eyes was unmistakable.

Her lips parted on a shaky breath. His eyes darkened in response.

She dropped her gaze to her hands knotting together nervously. "I haven't heard anything in a couple of minutes."

"Think they're gone?"

She wasn't sure. "I think we should get out of here."

As he started to return his P32 to its holster, she grabbed his wrist. His gaze whipped up to meet hers and all the heat between them that had begun to dissipate blazed back to life.

"Where do we go?" he asked, his voice a caress.

Her heart slammed wildly against her breastbone. "Not back to my house. Too many people." As the words spilled from her mouth, she realized they sounded like an invitation.

How do I get you alone?

His gaze never left hers. "How far is the cabin?"

"A fifteen-minute hike over the mountain." If she somehow had enough breath left to make the journey.

"Let's risk it. I don't think they're going to shoot

at us, and if they do, we're both armed and have a chance of beating them back until you can get your family here."

She managed a weak smile. "They've handled creeps like the SSU before. They can do it again."

He smiled briefly, before his eyes grew serious again. "Ready?"

She nodded and stood, taking a quick look around as she made a show of dusting the sand from her jeans. The woods around them weren't silent, exactly—birds, squirrels and other creatures flitted or crept about, as usual—but those noises were reassuring in a way. Earlier, when she'd heard the twigs snap, she'd also noticed the preternatural silence in the woods around them, nature's response to an intruder.

She didn't feel anyone out there anymore. The hair on the back of her neck lay flat and undisturbed.

She reached down, offering her hand to Evan. "Let's go."

He took her hand and let her help him to his feet, his fingers lingering against hers a second longer than necessary. Once again, his green eyes went dark.

But he let go of her hand and gestured toward the woods ahead. "Lead the way."

Her heart still racing like a thoroughbred, she started hiking up the mountain, Evan at her heels.

Chapter Five

"This is my fault." Evan peered through the curtains in the cabin's front room. "I should've thought it through—"

"Because crazy people generally stalk you?" Megan stood nearby, her hand on the butt of her Ruger. Big gun for a woman her size, but he was pretty sure she could handle it. He knew she'd held back on the hike, trying not to push his endurance.

Given how winded he felt, he had no room to feel insulted. "Crazy people don't generally stalk me," he denied. "But the past few weeks, I've had the feeling I'm being watched."

"You may be right." She crossed to the other window and looked out, the midday sun burnishing her hair until it glowed like flames. "What do they want? To shut you up?"

"I don't know. I'm not sure who's behind it."

"The tat suggests it's the SSU."

"I don't think it was the SSU following me in North Carolina," he disagreed, remembering the faces of the men he'd seen trailing his steps back home. Older faces, nondescript but alert. Not making themselves conspicuous but not appearing concerned about being spotted, either. "CIA, maybe."

Her gaze slanted toward him, glittering with wariness. "CIA seems a little—"

"Over-the-top? I know. And I guess it could have been any of the intelligence services, including the Pentagon's."

"Why would they cover up what happened to Vince—if your theory is right?" She shook her head. "MacLear is gone. Barton Reid is under indictment—"

"And for years, MacLear was one of the government's most trusted security contractors, despite running illegal operations right under their noses. Heads rolled when MacLear went under. How many more will roll if we can prove the SSU colluded with a high-level State Department official to kill a U.S. serviceman?"

"I don't see anyone out there," she said finally. "And we're wasting time holed up here, jumping every time a squirrel runs up a tree." She let the curtains fall and turned to look at him. "I'm going down to the marina and see if someone down there can give me a ride back to my place to pick up my car."

"No." He intercepted her as she headed for the door.

"No?" The fiery look she gave him would have

incinerated most men. He felt a little singed on the edges himself. "We're not partners. You don't get a say in what I do or where I go."

He moved out of her way, unable to argue with her point. She didn't trust him enough to consider him a partner. And considering the things he was still keeping from her, the suspicions about her husband he wasn't ready to share, he couldn't blame her for having doubts.

As she opened the door and stepped onto the porch, he said, "At least let me drive you home."

She paused at the edge of the steps. "Are you going to try to talk me into handing over those letters to you?"

"Yes."

Her lips curved slightly. "Probably won't work."

He arched his eyebrows. Probably? That was progress.

The trip back to her house was filled with silence, but it wasn't tense or uncomfortable. Now and then Megan gave him terse directions from the marina to the twisty road winding through the woods to her house, but mostly she just gazed through the windshield, a thoughtful look on her freckled face.

He struggled with the urge to watch her instead of the road, to his consternation. He'd never let a woman derail him from his work. He loved women, loved being with them. But he knew better than to give a relationship the starring role in his life. He'd seen what that kind of madness could do to a person. He'd seen the destruction when everything went wrong.

And it always went wrong, sooner or later.

Megan Randall was an attractive woman. Not a beauty—she was a mass of flaws, from her too-snub nose to her freckled complexion, her slight underbite to her flyaway hair. Her personality had its own problems, from her prickly independence to her flash-fire temper.

But he kept finding his gaze gravitating toward her, drawn like a bee to honeysuckle. It was almost a relief to pull into the driveway at the side of her house.

By now, all of the policemen had left; only a single vehicle remained, the Dodge Charger Rick Cooper drove. Megan got out of his car the second he pulled to a stop and strode forward with a jerk of her head, her hair swinging in a red arc. It was all the invitation he was going to get, he realized as she circled toward the back door.

He moved the rental car over, so that it sat behind Megan's car instead of her brother's, and cut the engine. He hurried after her, catching up at the door.

They found Rick in the kitchen, on his phone. He looked up at them, his dark eyebrows lifting. "She just got back. Yeah, safe and sound. Talk to you later."

"Were you about to send out a search party?" Megan asked, her voice tinged with resignation.

"We were considering it," Rick admitted. "It was Jesse's idea—I kept telling them you were a big girl and could take care of yourself."

"I bet." Megan gave him a little shove as she walked past him toward the cabinets. "Who cleaned up?"

"Isabel and Shannon came by to check on you, and they figured the last thing you'd want to see was a mess waiting for you when you got back. Where'd you go?"

"Walked Pike home," she said with a wry look at Evan. "Then he drove me back here. You want to have lunch with us?"

Trying to feed him again, Evan thought, smiling.

"Thanks, but Amanda and I were planning to try that new Thai place in Borland for lunch, so I'll be shoving off." He nodded politely to Evan, although Evan could tell that he wasn't any more inclined to offer his trust than his sister was.

He waited for Megan to tell Rick about their experience with the hidden stalker in the woods, but she let her brother go without saying a word.

"You're not going to tell him about what happened at the creek?" he asked her once Rick was gone.

"We didn't see a stalker. I can't say for sure there

was anyone out there." Her bulldog chin jutted stubbornly.

"You mean you don't want your family putting you in a cage somewhere to keep you safe."

"Would you?"

"No," he admitted. But it might be nice to have someone who gave a damn. "Listen, I know you were just being polite with the lunch invitation—"

Her lips quirked. "Afraid to try more of my cooking?"

"Should I be?"

"Probably," she admitted with a laugh. "Vince didn't marry me for my culinary skills." Her laughter faded, and her expression darkened. "I'm going to take a look at the letters."

Excitement darted through him. "Today?"

She nodded. "I don't remember anything odd in them, but I haven't reread the last few letters he sent before his death."

That was surprising, he thought. "Why not?"

"Too painful a reminder, I guess." She looked as if she had just admitted a shameful weakness.

"If it's too painful now, I can—"

"No," she interrupted sharply. "I'll read them. They're personal and I'm not ready to share them with anyone else."

"With me, you mean."

"With anyone." She shook her hair away from her face. "Man, this place is quiet without Patton around."

"He seems happy here." Evan went with the

change of subject even though he wanted to press the point about the letters. Megan wasn't the sort to be pushed, so trying to nudge her back to the subject would do him no good. "You've even managed to train some manners into him."

"He's a smart boy. He's been a godsend these past four years." She sighed. "The lunch invitation stands. I'm not such a bad cook I can't grill a cheese sandwich."

"Why don't I take you out somewhere for lunch?" he suggested. "As a thank-you."

Her brow furrowed. "For what?"

"For agreeing to look at the letters."

She shook her head. "I'm doing that for myself, not you. If someone did murder Vince, he needs to pay before he kills some other soldier who's in the wrong place at the wrong time."

Evan wished he thought Vince was as innocent as Megan clearly believed. But in his experience, innocent people weren't usually targeted for assassination. Vince must have known something he shouldn't, and since none of his superior officers had mentioned his coming to them with suspicions, he must have kept quiet about what he knew.

Vince's unit had worked side by side with MacLear contractors. Had he made a deal with the devil?

"I was serious about taking you to lunch," he said aloud. "Anywhere you want."

"I'm not hungry. I want to go read those letters."

"Okay." He started toward the door. "You'll call me if you find anything?"

"I will," she said.

He turned in the doorway, reluctant to leave her alone, and not just because he knew there were people already in Gossamer Ridge who showed no compunction about breaking and entering at will. "You'll be careful, right?"

The look she gave him would have made a lesser man wilt, but he stood his ground. Finally, her expression cleared and she nodded. "I'll be careful." She patted the Ruger holstered at her hip. "Plus, armed."

He took some comfort in the thought.

He left her house and headed back toward the lake, planning to stop at the gas station food mart near the turn-off. But halfway to the crossroads, he found himself passing the graveyard where he'd first seen Megan earlier that morning. Had it been such a short time ago?

He pulled the Taurus off the road and got out, entering the tiny cemetery through a wrought-iron gate that creaked loudly as he opened it. He found Vince Randall's gravestone quickly, as there were only a handful of graves.

No flowers, he noted with surprise.

He crouched by the stone. "What were you into, Randall? Is it something that's going to come back to haunt her, too?"

The grave remained silent.

NIGHT HAD FALLEN, VELVETY BLUE, outside the large windows of the agents' bullpen. At her desk in the corner, Megan looked up from her husband's letters and saw she was the only one left in the room. The growl in her stomach reminded her she'd skipped lunch and, so far, dinner.

But she'd made it through most of her husband's letters from his last deployment, and one thing had become clear: Vince's opinion of Evan Pike had changed considerably over the final few weeks of his life.

Pike went to the mats for Blake and Tompkins, Vince had written about two weeks before his death, describing a situation where top brass had given a couple of infantrymen a hard time about a live-fire incident resulting in the death of a villager. Pike had apparently argued forcefully in the soldiers' defense, pointing out the danger the so-called "innocent" villager had actually posed to the soldiers.

There were other incidents, other words of grudging praise for Evan Pike from Vince. Megan had read all of these letters before, so why hadn't she noticed the change in her husband's opinion of Pike? Had his earlier frustrations with the Pentagon liaison so colored her opinion of him that she hadn't seen the subtle changes in Vince's mentions of the man?

She set aside Vince's letters for a moment and picked up the one-sheeter Shannon had left on her desk with a big grin—a typewritten preliminary summary of Cooper Security's background check on Evan Pike. "Just the job stuff so far," Shannon had warned as she handed off the information. "We're still working on his pre-Pentagon life."

Everything he'd told her checked out so far, including his "divorce," as he called it, from the Pentagon. These days, Evan was doing some freelance legal consulting for a Defense Department contractor based in Norfolk, Virginia. He currently lived in a modest apartment complex in a community just over the state line in North Carolina.

Quite a comedown from being a hotshot Pentagon lawyer, she thought.

Penance for his perceived sins?

Setting aside the background check, she took the letter from Vince to the scanner and copied it to her work computer, as she'd done for all the others. She replaced it in the shoe box where she stored the letters and pulled out the last one. It was dated four years and three weeks ago—just two days before Vince's death.

After a few paragraphs of more personal conversation, his letter turned to his life in Kaziristan. She settled deeper into her chair and read as he described a trip to the capital city of Tablis.

People are everywhere. You get used to wide-open spaces out in the wilds, so it's a shock to be suddenly drowning in a sea of people. The rural parts are so primitive in so many ways that you forget how cosmopolitan Tablis can be. Europeans, Arabs, Kaziris, Africans and Asians all mingle in the streets and bazaars, the air filled with chatter in a dozen different languages. In some ways, I wish you could be here to experience it. In other ways, I'm glad you're not. It's a dangerous place. You can't ever let yourself forget it.

Megan blinked back tears. She wished she'd been there, too. Maybe she could have seen something, heard something—

She released a soft growl of frustration. Madness lay that way. She could drive herself crazy with what-ifs.

She read the rest of the letter, pausing at an odd passage near the end.

You should be receiving a package in the next few weeks. Look for it.

Package? She hadn't received any packages from Vince that close to his death. What had he been talking about?

Her desk phone rang, so loud in the quiet bullpen that it jangled her nerves. She grabbed the receiver. "Megan Cooper."

"I had a feeling you'd still be there." Evan Pike's

low voice rumbled through the phone line. "Still reading letters?"

"Just finishing up," she admitted. "The only thing I've discovered is that Vince had planned to send me a package. But I never got it."

"A package?" Evan sounded intrigued.

"It might be nothing," she warned.

"Have you eaten dinner yet?"

Her stomach growled at the thought. "Not yet."

"I'm a few blocks from your office, at some barbecue joint. Want to join me?"

"No, that's okay—" Her eyes felt puffy and raw, and with her melancholy mood, she wouldn't make a good dinner companion.

"So I'll get takeout and meet you at the office," he said.

"Pike—"

"You skipped lunch—not healthy."

"And barbecue is?"

He ignored the question. "Chicken, pork or beef?"

She sighed. "Pork. A sandwich is fine. And slaw. Tea to drink—sweet tea."

"Be there in about fifteen minutes." He hung up.

Megan finished scanning the last of Vince's letters and saved them to her work computer. After putting the physical letters back in the shoe box to be stored in the safe, she copied the scans onto a flash drive and slipped it into her purse. That gave her two copies of the letters besides the actual paper originals. To be safe, she also uploaded a copy to the company's web archive.

As she returned the box to the small documents safe, she saw headlights flash against the bullpen windows. She glanced at her watch. Evan so soon?

She turned out the lights in the communal office as she left, since she was finished there, and headed downstairs before he set off an alarm trying to get in the building.

But the dark-clad figure standing in front of the main entrance doors wasn't Evan Pike.

And he was holding a Glock, fitted with a silencer, that made her Ruger look like a toy.

Megan backed into the shadows of the darkened foyer, whispering a quick prayer of thanks that she'd bypassed turning on the lights. The security floodlights outside were bright enough to turn the glass front of the security office into a virtual mirror, hiding her backward scuttle out of sight.

She tugged her cell phone from the front pocket of her purse and dialed Jesse's cell phone.

He answered on the third ring. "Hey, Meggie, tell me you're not still at the office."

"I'm still at the office, and I'm not alone." She peeked around the corner, wondering why the black-clad intruder hadn't already tried to enter. She told her brother what she'd seen outside. "I saw just one guy, but I doubt he's alone. They haven't tried to come in yet—"

"Maybe trying to bypass the alarm," Jesse

growled. She heard movement on his end of the phone—he was probably already on his way to the door.

"Keep it stealthy," she warned. "If you don't spook them, we might be able to catch them in the act."

"Can you get to the walk-in safe without being seen?" The roar of an engine on Jesse's side of the call told her he was already in his SUV.

"I think so." Not that she was happy at the thought of holing up like a coward while her family took care of the intruders. She risked another look around the corner. The man in black was no longer there, but she saw the flash of headlights slice through the darkness outside. A car was entering the parking lot.

Evan! She hadn't called to warn him!

"I have to hang up. I'll call back." She hung up the phone and scrolled through her call log—Evan Pike had tried to call her a couple of days earlier, hadn't he? She'd ignored the call, but maybe his number was still listed—

There. She hit the respond button and waited.

But Evan didn't answer.

THE SOUND OF HIS PHONE RINGING seemed shockingly loud in the warm night air. Evan paused in mid-step to fish his phone from his pocket and nearly jumped out of his skin when something whistled past his ear and smacked into the ornamental pear tree five yards away.

He hadn't heard anything but a faint blatting sound, but he knew what that whistling noise meant as it whizzed by his head. He'd heard the sound too many times in Kaziristan.

Someone was shooting at him.

Chapter Six

Tossing the drinks and the bag of barbecue sandwiches aside, Evan dropped and rolled for cover behind a boxwood hedge lining the walkway in front of Cooper Security.

No second shot came, though his phone kept ringing, giving away his position. He silenced the phone, his breath coming in short, hard gasps. He forced his breathing to slow, as well, trying to tuck himself farther under the boxwood hedge, which definitely wasn't trimmed to accommodate a man his size.

He waited, listening, his entire body alert. He had known nights like this before, nights when the al Adar raids had struck with fury, if not great power. As a civilian, he'd been pushed to the rear, shielded behind the armed men running toward danger instead of away. It had been a humbling experience.

One he'd hoped never to repeat.

He shifted position so that he could retrieve the Kel-Tec P32 holstered at his ankle. The heft of the compact gun gave him a little shot of confidence, and he scooted closer to the building, hoping for a better angle.

The first flush of reaction eased, clearing his mind.

He needed to warn Megan.

As he reached for his cell phone, it buzzed again, a muted vibration against his hip. He pulled it from his pocket and checked the display. It was Megan's cell phone number.

He took a chance and answered. "Megan, there are armed men outside Cooper Security."

"I know." Her low drawl jolted through him like a bracing shot of whiskey. "Are you okay?"

"I'm pinned near the front door. Can't see the shooters."

"Stay put. Jesse's coming—I'm sure he'll bring backup."

"They've already shot at me once."

The tenor of her voice changed. "Are you hurt?"

In any other circumstance, he might take pleasure in her concern. "No, but I'm a sitting duck where I am."

He heard her soft exhalation. "Which side of the door?"

"Your right."

"I'm going to open the door. That'll trigger a loud alarm, which may distract them long enough for you to slip inside. You ready?"

"As I'll ever be." He darted a quick look over the

hedge, his grip tightening on the P32. He spotted several black-clad men at the side of the building, gathered near the side wall. "They're messing with something down the building—"

"Trying to cut power," she said. "But we have backup power. Opening the door now."

He heard a rattle as she unlocked the door. The second it swung open, a deafening klaxon pierced the night, sending birds soaring from their perches in the surrounding trees and drawing the attention of the men in black.

Evan dived for the open door and scrambled inside, pushing to his feet. "They're coming!" he warned.

She locked the door behind her and grabbed his hand, pulling him toward a dark stairwell, her short legs having surprisingly little trouble keeping up with his longer strides. Behind them, the door shuddered with the intruders' attempts to break the glass.

"It's bullet-resistant," Megan breathed, "but it won't hold against a sustained onslaught."

Great, he thought.

They raced up the darkened stairway, his feet stumbling on the unfamiliar terrain. Two floors up, they burst into a shadowy corridor lit only by emergency exit lights.

"This way," Megan said, tugging his hand as she started to sprint down the gloomy hallway. She led him into a central room with a large vault at one end. "Turn around," she ordered.

He did as she asked. He heard her punching numbers into a keypad in the wall, then a loud hiss, as if a giant vacuum-sealed container had come unsealed.

Megan tugged his arm. "In here."

Following her into the narrow vault, he found himself surrounded by shelves full of archived materials—boxes of files, stacks of labeled videotapes and compact discs, even a few pieces of what looked like priceless artwork—paintings, sketches, sculptures and statuary.

"You never saw any of this," Megan warned. "Not where we keep it or what's inside. Understand? Our clients depend on us for complete discretion."

He nodded, realizing how narrow the vault was. It wasn't meant to accommodate more than one person at a time. He could barely breathe without his rib cage brushing Megan's breasts.

"Can you get a cell signal out of here?" he asked doubtfully, looking at the solid construction of the vault.

Megan shook her head. "But this is where Jesse told me to go, so he'll look for me here."

"Will we run out of air?"

"Not anytime soon. There's a vent that pipes in air as long as the electricity holds, and as long as those guys out there don't cut the auxiliary power—"

The dim emergency lights near the ceiling went out, plunging them into utter darkness.

"You were saying?" Evan murmured, fighting the urge to escape the vault for somewhere less airtight.

She caught his hand, her fingers twining with his. "Wait."

He heard a soft thud and the dim lights flashed on. Feeling a rush of air across his face, he took a deep breath. "Auxiliary power?"

"Yep." She still held his hand, he noticed, her small fingers warm and firm between his own. "How did they know to come here?" she asked.

"I don't know."

"You haven't talked to anyone since you left my house, have you?" Her tone was urgent.

"I stopped by the marina on the way back to the cabin to pick up some snacks, but I didn't say anything but 'thanks' and 'see you later.'"

"They came straight here." Her brow furrowed. "And the only people who know about the letters being here are my family. I didn't tell anyone else what was in the box."

"How sure are you that you can trust your other coworkers? I mean, if they saw you with a box—"

"It's not that uncommon." She waved her hand around the vault. "We often bring items here to store for clients, so nobody would have blinked an eye."

"But if they already knew what to look for—"

She tilted her head back to look into his eyes. "I trust the people I work with. They've all been through hell and back, in one way or the other. We've vetted them all so closely we can probably tell you how many freckles they have and where."

"So if not someone here at Cooper Security, then who?"

Her gaze narrowing, she let go of his hand. "*You* knew."

Anger snapped through him. "So I'm back to being a suspect again? Really?"

She sighed, her breath warm on his neck, eliciting a shudder of pure masculine awareness. "No."

The klaxons outside, still faintly audible through the thick steel door, silenced suddenly. Megan slid her hand into his again, and he closed his fingers tightly around hers.

"I hope that means your brothers are here."

"Me, too," she admitted. She let go of his hand and pulled her Ruger from her hip holster, checking the clip. He followed her lead, making sure there was a round chambered in the P32.

He heard faint noises on the other side of the door. Megan gestured for him to take the left side, while she set up on the right. His breath felt like fire in his lungs, but he willed himself to remain calm and steady.

The door seal popped and air seeped into the vault, cool on his cheeks.

"They're gone." The deep voice outside the door belonged to Jesse Cooper. "You okay?"

"Did anyone get inside?" Megan pushed the door out slowly. Jesse and another man stood near the vault door.

"They managed to cut the power and banged the hell out of the front door, but they fled into the woods when we arrived. There's a whole posse of Coopers after them. J.D. is downstairs trying to figure out how hard it'll be to restore power." Jesse looked surprised to see Evan emerge from the vault behind Megan. "That's *your* Taurus in the lot?"

Evan nodded. "And if you come across a bag of barbecue sandwiches, that's our dinner."

Megan began to laugh, the tone a little uncontrolled.

"Any idea who those guys were?" the other man asked. It was one of Megan's brothers, Evan was pretty sure—he remembered meeting him at the motel—but the name escaped him.

"Silencers, big guns—almost has to be the SSU," Megan said. "Any idea how many there were?"

"I saw at least three before I made it inside," Evan said.

"We counted five running for the woods," Jesse said.

"I'm surprised you came in here instead of going after them," Megan said.

Jesse ruffled her hair, making her grimace. "I told you I'd be here to get you, and I was afraid you'd shoot anyone else who tried to come in."

Her lips quirked in a half smile, she put her Ruger in its holster and gave her brother a quick hug. "Thanks."

"They seemed determined to get in here," Jesse growled. "What do they think you're going to find in those letters?"

"I've been through all of them. The only odd thing I found was that Vince sent me a package I never got."

"And you didn't find that odd before?" Jesse asked.

The bleak look on Megan's face made Evan's chest ache. "That letter came a few days after the casualty assistance officers informed me of Vince's death. Those days are a blur."

"Did he say what was in the package?" Evan asked.

Megan shook her head. "I wonder what happened to it."

"Maybe that's a good place to look next," Evan suggested.

"Did either of you say anything to anyone about the letters?" Megan asked her brothers.

"Just the family. And you know none of them are going to let something like that slip." The other brother took a hitching step toward Megan and Rick remembered his name. Wade Cooper, a former Marine Corps captain who'd been discharged due to injury. Took a bullet in the knee in a battle three years earlier.

"I think maybe we need to take a listening device detector to my place," Megan said.

Evan hadn't even thought of that possibility, but of course it made sense. They knew someone had been in her house earlier that day, long enough to steal the other letters. They could have planted any number of listening devices around the bungalow. Megan had mentioned bringing the box of letters here to the office. A listening device could have picked up that conversation easily.

To think they'd been worried about that young cop overhearing them....

"Are the letters safe?" Wade asked.

"Yeah, they're in the small documents safe. And I've scanned them to the computer and uploaded to our secure web archive, as well. Plus, there's a copy on a flash drive in my purse." She patted the small black bag slung over her shoulder.

"Good thinking," Jesse said approvingly.

Megan shot him a wry look. "About time you realized I'm capable of it."

"You're not going to guilt me for worrying about you," Jesse shot back. "I haven't called the police yet. You want them in on this?"

"Well, that depends on whether or not the others manage to catch up with the intruders," Megan said drily.

As it turned out, the black-clad intruders had enough of a head start to evade their pursuers until they met up with a getaway vehicle parked on Ridge View Road about a quarter mile away. Rick Cooper met them downstairs with the bad news.

"They've learned from our previous skirmishes," he said with a grimace. "They can't beat us on our own playing field, so they've learned to build escape plans."

"I need people to stay here with me to guard the office until our security system techs can do the repairs," Jesse said. He addressed his cousins directly. "Can any of y'all stay, too? I don't want us to be outnumbered if any of these bastards decide to come back."

"I'm in," one of them drawled. Evan searched his mind for the name. J.D. The former navy man. Three other Coopers agreed—the twins and the one named Luke.

"I have to be at work early in the morning, so I'm going to have to beg off," one of the men said with regret. He was a big guy—a deputy, if Evan remembered correctly. "Sure you don't want to involve Maybridge PD? They're a good department."

"A small-town force isn't equipped to take on a private army, Aaron. You know that. We'd be putting them in unnecessary danger." Jesse turned to Megan. "You sure the two of you want to go back to your place alone?"

She exchanged looks with Evan, as if asking his opinion. He gave a quick nod. If she was right about a listening device at her place, he doubted the former MacLear operatives would be in a hurry to return there. The bug would do the work for them.

"I'll need a bug detector," Megan said.

"I'll get you outfitted," Wade said. Evan tried not to wince as he watched the man limp down the hall.

"Don't let him see your pity," Megan warned quietly.

Evan met her gaze. "No pity here. I was just thinking he must be one hell of a tough old leatherneck to be able to walk at all after taking a bullet to the kneecap."

Her eyes glimmered with pride. "He is."

Wade returned with an electronic device about the size of a cell phone. "Want my suggestion? Don't try to remove the bugs if you find them. Just leave them in place and don't say anything you don't want them to hear. We may be able to use the bugs to lure them into a trap if we play it right."

"Good idea," Evan said.

Megan grimaced. "I don't want to stay there with someone listening to me all the time. Maybe I'll come back and stand guard with the rest of you, at least for tonight."

"Let's find out whether or not there are even bugs there," Evan suggested, flattening his hand on her back and nudging her toward the door. She slanted a quick look at him, her gray eyes smoldering. Heat flooded through him, and he had to look away to keep from stumbling over his own feet.

Outside, he found the discarded bag of dinner on the ground near the boxwood hedge. He picked it up, finding the foil-wrapped sandwiches were still hot. "Probably still okay to eat, if you're hungry," he said with a grin.

"If we don't find any bugs at my place, I'll make some tea and we'll have a proper dinner." Her smile looked a little pinched around the edges.

But they didn't even get inside Megan's house before the device in her hand lit up, indicating the presence of a listening device somewhere within a twenty-five-yard radius.

Megan stopped on the porch and looked up at Evan, her expression sharp with anger. "Sons of bitches," she whispered.

Then her chin went up, her back straightened, and she unlocked her front door and went inside, like a Christian heading into the arena to face a hungry lion.

Evan squared his own shoulders and followed her inside.

"WE FOUND FIVE DEVICES," Megan told the others when she and Evan returned to the Cooper Security building about an hour later. "They weren't taking any chances."

One of the bugs had been in Megan's kitchen,

which explained how the black-clad intruders had known to look for the letters at Cooper Security.

"Why do they think the letters are so important?" Isabel's husband, Ben, asked.

"Because *I* think they're important," Evan answered.

"Who did you tell about your trip here?" Jesse asked.

"A couple of my former bosses at the Pentagon," he answered slowly, looking a little ill. "People I thought I could trust."

"You can't know they betrayed you on purpose," Isabel said. "Where did you tell them about it?"

"At Major Kinsley's office."

"Which could also be bugged," Megan said, picking up on her sister's point. "Did you specifically mention wanting to look at the letters Vince sent to me?"

"I did. Vince spent a lot of his downtime writing to you. I figured if he suspected anything, he might have told you something about it."

"Don't you think if he'd even hinted someone was gunning for him, Megan would have made a stink about it by now?" Wade asked, eyeing Evan with a hint of anger, as if he'd just accused Megan of obstructing justice.

"He might have said something Megan wouldn't have known was a clue."

"But you would?" Wade pressed.

"Maybe." Evan's jaw squared. "I think if we can

figure out what happened to the package Vince wrote you about, we'll be a step ahead."

"What if it's nothing but a pretty scarf he picked up at one of the bazaars in Tablis?" Megan countered, shaking her head. "I think if Vince knew he was in danger from someone at MacLear, he'd have told me outright, if only to make sure I could warn Rick about it."

"We should at least try to find it," Evan argued.

"You're right—we should. I just don't think we should get our hopes up that it's going to answer all our questions."

Evan sighed. "I'll be happy if it answers one or two."

"Do you even know where to look?" Jesse asked.

"I have an idea where to start." Megan had been pondering that question on the drive back to the office from her home. "If Vince got a package ready to send home, wouldn't someone in his unit know about it? I mean, it's not the kind of thing you could hide, and Vince didn't send a lot of packages home. He didn't like to deal with the rigmarole of shipping stuff from a war zone."

"Yeah, people in his unit would know about it," Jesse agreed. "You thinking about trying to track some of them down?"

She knew exactly where to start. "I need to drive over to Fort Benning and see what happened to the guys in his unit."

Chapter Seven

Megan's family stared at her as if she'd lost her mind.

"By yourself?" Jesse asked, his expression fierce.

She tried not to bristle, as it was a reasonable question, but Jesse's tone made her feel like a twelve-year-old. "I thought Pike might want to go with me."

Evan met the challenge in her gaze with wariness. "I'm not a favorite with that unit."

"We'll make it work." She ignored the skeptical look on her brothers' faces and turned to Isabel. "Can you get Patton out of the vet's office tomorrow? Have them put the charge on the credit card they have on file. I'll call from the road to let them know it's okay."

"Sure," Isabel agreed. "He can stay in the backyard and chase the rabbits that have been eating our lettuce plants."

"He might dig them up himself," Megan warned. She turned to Evan. "Come on. I'll follow you back to the cabin and help you pack your stuff."

Jesse followed them into the stairwell. "You're about to ask questions that may stir up a hornet's nest. You really sure you two want to do this?"

"Someone's trying damned hard to keep us from asking questions," Megan answered firmly, though her insides trembled at the thought of what she and Evan might be stepping into.

"I can go alone," Evan suggested.

Megan scowled at the look of approval in her brother's eyes. "You said yourself you're hardly a favorite with Vince's unit. You're not going to get the answers I will."

She saw her brother and Evan exchange a long look that made her want to punch them both.

"I'm not fragile and I'm not stupid. I know the dangers. I'll do what I can to keep them from coming to fruition. Okay? Do I need to apply for permission in writing?"

"She can do this," Evan said to Jesse, earning her brother's frown.

"Can and should are two different things."

"Come on, Pike," Megan said firmly. She started down the stairs, leaving Evan to catch up.

"Stay in touch!" Jesse called down behind them.

"Will do," Evan answered for her, coming level with her as they reached the ground floor. He walked with her as far as her little blue Jeep Wrangler. "Are you sure about this? Here, you're surrounded by your family for backup—"

"And they'll back me up out there, too, if I call

them," she argued, even though part of her felt as if she were cutting some invisible cord tethering her to earth. Since Vince's death, and her full time return to the Cooper fold, she'd become used to having her family around for comfort and support. "You don't have to go with me if you don't want to."

"No way are you leaving me out of this." His jaw squared stubbornly, the pale blue moonlight caressing the angles and planes of his handsome face. To her consternation, her fingers itched to follow those same lines.

"Okay." Her voice came out hoarse and unsteady. "Can I bunk at the cabin?"

His eyes widened. "Tonight?"

"If we leave at first light, we can be at Fort Benning by midmorning. We may even be able to get the information we want and be back here before midnight. It'll save time if I'm already at the cabin."

He still looked troubled.

"Not an early riser?" she prodded.

He made a face. "I kept combat hours for three years. I think I can manage getting up before dawn."

"Then what's the problem?"

He looked at her, his expression thoughtful. "If you don't have a problem with it, I sure don't." He stepped back to let her open her car door.

I don't have a problem with it, she assured herself, even though her mind was already flashing forward to where she was going to bunk down and how hard it would be to drift off to sleep while her mind kept replaying the way moonlight had etched Evan's face into a thing of rare beauty.

She made herself think of Vince on the drive to the cabin, visualizing the craggy masculinity of his features and the raw male power of his body pressed against hers. As a familiar ache of longing began to bloom in the center of her chest, she nursed the sensation, let it grow until she was nearly in tears by the time she pulled up in the parking area outside the Gossamer Mountain cabin.

Evan's rental car pulled up behind her vehicle. He joined her behind the Jeep. "I didn't see anyone following you."

She cleared the ache from her throat. "But did anyone follow *you?*"

"I don't think so. But let's bring everything inside the house, just in case. I don't want anyone rifling through our things without our knowing about it." He patted the Wrangler's back window. "Keys?"

She handed him the keys and he retrieved her duffel. "You should pack a bag for tomorrow, in case we have to stay somewhere overnight," she said as they climbed the cabin steps.

He unlocked the front door of the cabin, but as

Megan started to push through, he caught her arm. "Let's be sure we don't have any visitors."

Stupid of her not to think of that possibility herself. She nodded, easing her Ruger from the holster. "Ready?" she asked softly.

He wiggled the butt of the P32 at her and nodded.

They went in quietly, checking room by room until they were satisfied that Evan hadn't received any unexpected visitors during the time he was gone. The bug-detector showed no sign of listening devices, either. While he locked up behind them, Megan took her things into the smaller of the cabin's two bedrooms. It had bunk beds instead of the larger queen-sized bed in Evan's room, but it was a place to sleep and had its own small bathroom. She'd slept in worse places.

"Like where?" Evan asked later after she assured him over a dinner of reheated barbecue sandwiches that the room was a luxury spa compared to some of the places she'd stayed.

"When I was working for Homeland Security, they sent us to Afghanistan for training. I slept on a dirt floor in a little village near the Tajikistan border. I don't think I've ever been that cold in my life."

"You worked at Homeland Security?" Evan looked surprised.

"That wasn't in your research on my family?"

He shook his head. "I guess maybe Homeland

Security is like *Fight Club*. First rule of Homeland Security is—"

"You don't talk about Homeland Security," she finished in tandem with him. "My job wasn't undercover or anything. I was an analyst. Mostly I went through reams and reams of intel, trying to piece together any obvious links. The Afghanistan trip was an anomaly, believe me."

"How long did you work for Homeland Security?"

"I started not too long before I married Vince— right out of college. I lived in D.C. for a year, then when I married Vince, they reassigned me to work as a liaison with the Alabama Department of Homeland Security, since Vince was stationed at Fort Benning about two hours away from the office in Montgomery." She grimaced at the memory. "A lot of the time, I'd stay at a motel near my office during the week and return home to the base on weekends."

"That had to be rough on a new marriage."

"We made it work. Vince was deployed a lot of the time, so it wasn't like it mattered where I was staying."

Evan shook his head. "Don't know how you did it. These days, marriages end in divorce for no reason at all—"

"We loved each other," she said. "We wanted to be together, so we made it work."

He crumpled the foil wrapper of his sandwich into a tight ball. "That simple, huh?"

"I never said it was simple." She shot him a wry smile.

"We should probably get some shut-eye," he suggested, gathering the remains of their dinner.

"Thank you."

He looked up at her, his brow furrowed. "For what?"

"For dinner. And for coming with me."

"This investigation was mine to begin with. Thank you for joining it." His voice softened, and he took a step closer to her. "I know it's making you relive a lot of memories that give you pain. I'm sorry for that."

"If someone murdered my husband, he has to pay," she said simply, telling herself the fire licking at her belly had everything to do with outrage and nothing to do with how close Evan was standing, close enough that she could feel the heat radiating from his big, rangy body.

She escaped to the small bedroom for a quick shower to save them time in the morning. And if the water was a little cooler than she normally liked, that was purely a coincidence.

ONCE THEY REACHED HIGHWAY 231, heading southeast toward the Georgia state line, the drive to Columbus was easier than Evan had assumed—a good thing, since sleep had been harder to come by than he'd expected after the long, eventful day before.

Megan Randall's smoky gray eyes and fiery soul had chased him through his dreams, as tantalizing as a mythical siren. He gave up on pretending he didn't find her exciting and attractive, since he wasn't fooling anyone, especially not himself. It wasn't as if there was anything he could do about it anyway. She was about the worst prospect for a no-strings fling he could think of, and no-strings was all he could manage these days.

She sat with her bare feet propped up on the dashboard of the rented Taurus, her attention focused on the tablet computer resting against her bare knees. He'd been alarmed when she'd emerged from her bedroom early that morning wearing a pair of hiking shorts that hit her mid-thigh— modest by most standards but nothing but temptation for Evan. Her sleeveless cotton T-shirt also covered more than it bared, but the cut skimmed her curves like a caress, reminding Evan that for all her wiry strength, she was still a woman blessed by nature with tantalizing curves and valleys that tempted a man to explore.

"The names that keep coming up again and again in his letters are Delgado, Raines and Gates," Megan said aloud, not looking up from the tablet.

Rafe Delgado, Tyrone Raines and Donald Gates,

Evan thought, remembering those three with great clarity, despite having been stateside for over three years. He'd spent his days among those men, trying to win their trust and respect. Sometimes it had worked. Sometimes it hadn't.

He'd gotten along well enough with Raines. Delgado hadn't warmed up at all, and Gates had seemed entirely distrustful. "How do we know any of them are still around Fort Benning after all this time?" he asked.

"We don't," she admitted. "I should have called ahead."

"You can call now," he said, glancing at the dashboard clock. It was eight-forty-five. The personnel office should have been open long before now.

To his surprise, she gave him a quick look full of apprehension. He'd begun to see her as such a fierce, fearless warrior of a woman that he'd almost forgotten how painful this endeavor must surely be for her, reconnecting with the people she'd once considered friends, even family. The army engendered more than just a "band of brothers" philosophy among the soldiers. The soldiers' families, as well, formed cohesive bonds of shared sacrifice and constant awareness of how fragile life really was.

Her shoulders squaring, she pulled out her phone and made a call, typing notes on the tablet computer as she spoke to the person on the other end of the line. When she hung up, she looked up at Evan with a triumphant smile.

"That was Allie Dawson—we used to live two houses away from each other," she said. "We're lucky I got her. I probably wouldn't have gotten this much otherwise. Two are still in the army—Delgado and Raines. They're both still at Benning. Gates is out. She couldn't share any further information, of course."

"But maybe Delgado and Raines will know?"

"Exactly." Her smile lingered. "Man, it was great talking to Allie again. We lost touch after Vince died."

He had a feeling she'd cut ties deliberately, out of self-preservation. He'd seen it happen before.

"Allie's going to meet us at the gate to get us in on visitor's passes. She said we should be able to catch Rafe and Tyrone when they break for mess." Megan's smile faded suddenly.

"Something wrong?" he asked.

Her mouth curved in a brief, bleak smile. "I didn't think I'd ever go back to Fort Benning again."

"You don't have to if you don't want to."

She shook her head, her chin jutting sharply. "I'm going. We're going to see this through."

But even though her whole body vibrated with determination, Evan could see, in the pain-tinted shadows in her gray eyes, just how much the effort was costing her.

ALLIE DAWSON WAS AS SWEET-NATURED and pretty as Megan remembered, though perhaps ten pounds plumper. "Still trying to lose weight from baby number two!" she said with a rueful smile as she ran her hand over the remains of her baby bump.

"Two?" Megan tamped down a sense of envy and asked to see pictures, which Allie promptly supplied. While Megan oohed and ahhed over the photos of two undeniably cute tow-headed tykes, she noticed Allie was eying Evan Pike with a speculative gleam in her eyes. She always had been something of a matchmaker, trying to pair up all the single soldiers with girls she knew from town. Now that Megan was unattached, Allie probably saw her as fair game, especially after four years of widowhood.

If she had ever heard of Evan from her husband, she showed no sign of hostility toward him.

"So, what are you doing now?" she asked Megan eagerly. "Still with Homeland Security?"

"I'm working for my brother. He started Cooper Security about four years ago, so he brought me in as an analyst. Now I'm also doing field work."

Allie's eyes widened. "Is it as exciting as it sounds?"

"Not really," Megan answered with a wry laugh. Next to her, Evan shifted in his seat, looking uncomfortable. Didn't like girl talk? Most men didn't, she knew. She herself could take it only in small doses.

Before long, Allie's lunch break arrived, giving poor Evan the reprieve he'd probably been praying for. "Delgado and Raines usually eat together at one of the main base restaurants," Allie told Megan, adding a bright wink. "I've got a date with my hubby at our favorite Italian place off base." She walked them out of the visitor center, eliciting a promise from Megan to stay in touch more often.

Fort Benning was like a small city unto itself, with almost every amenity a soldier could hope to find in any small metropolitan area, including an enormous post exchange, banks, a vet clinic, a hospital and even a movie theater. Megan and Evan spent the better part of the next twenty minutes going from one on-base restaurant to another, looking for Delgado or Raines.

They found Rafe Delgado sitting alone at a Mexican restaurant at a table not far from the door. He caught Megan's eye and blinked with surprise, a grin spreading across his face as he recognized her. But as they crossed to his table, he spotted Evan, his expression darkening to suspicion immediately.

Megan sighed. Evan had expected that kind of greeting from Delgado. It couldn't be helped.

"What on earth are you doing here, Mrs. Randall?"

"Came to see you and Tyrone. Is he around?"

"He just got his order—Ty!" Delgado waved the tall, rawboned young black man over. Raines's eyes widened in surprise at the sight of Evan, but he showed no signs of hostility, to Megan's relief. Raines set his food on the table where they sat and bent to give Megan a kiss on the cheek.

"What are you doing back here in gruntsville, Meggie?" Raines sat across from her.

"I'm looking for a little information." In vague terms, Megan told them about the package her husband had mentioned in one of his last letters. "Did either of you see anything like that—a package Vince wanted to send me?"

The two men exchanged looks.

"What?" Megan prodded.

"He gave a package to someone in the unit to send out for him, about a day before he was shot," Raines answered. Delgado, she noticed, was still eyeing Evan with wariness. Probably why Evan was letting her take the lead in the questioning, despite the tense energy she felt radiating from him.

"Do you remember who?" she asked.

"Gates," both men said at the same time.

"Sarge seemed to think Gates had what it took to be officer material if he'd just put in a little effort, but Ducky wasn't ambitious," Raines told her.

"So Sarge tried to jump-start a little fire in his belly," Delgado added. "Gave him extra duties, tried to instill a sense of pride in accomplishment." He darted his gaze toward Evan. "Sarge didn't think leadership should be the rich cat's domain."

Evan's lips flattened with annoyance, but he let Delgado's pointed barb pass unremarked.

"Did Gates post the package?"

"He said he did."

"You didn't see him do it?" Evan spoke for the first time.

Both men's gazes whipped up to him, and even Raines showed a hint of careful wariness. "Come on, Pentagon, you know we didn't babysit each other. People had duties and we expected they did them," he said.

"Who was the post officer at the time?" Megan asked.

"Corporal Donegan," Evan answered. "The captain put him in charge of package posting."

"'Cause he worked for FedEx when he wasn't on active duty," Delgado added. "He was a reservist."

"He's actually from Georgia," Raines added helpfully. "Up around LaGrange, I think. I think he's off active duty now—you might be able to track him down."

"I have his cell phone number," Delgado said, digging in his pocket for his wallet. "He said he might want to sell his '78 Camaro and I've been lookin' for one of those."

Evan pulled out his cell phone and took the number Delgado gave him. "Thanks."

Delgado's expression shifted to curiosity. "Is this just about finding that package?"

Megan darted a quick look at Evan. Meeting her

gaze, he gave a small nod. "Did either of y'all ever hear rumors about Vince's death?"

Delgado and Raines exchanged glances. "What kind of rumors?" Delgado asked.

"That maybe it wasn't an enemy sniper that shot him."

Raines toyed with the remains of his lunch. "Nobody in al Adar could've made that shot."

"That's what I heard," she said, not elaborating on who'd told her. Their attitude toward Evan had begun to soften to indifference to his presence, at best. She didn't want to put them back on edge by letting them know that Evan was the impetus behind this interview.

But their gazes went to Evan anyway. "You finally got your head out of your backside long enough to figure it out?"

He inclined his head as if admitting defeat. "I should have listened to the scuttlebutt."

"You said we were letting grief overcome our good sense." Delgado mimicked Evan's neutral accent.

"Why didn't y'all tell *me?*" Megan asked pointedly. "I came down here to greet you when you returned home. You could have told me then."

"For what?" Raines asked. "Pentagon and his buddies had already made the pronouncement. KIA."

Killed in Action. Just thinking about the words took Megan back to that terrible day four years ago when the notification officers brought her the news of her husband's death. She'd always known it was a possibility, though in a peacekeeping action like Kaziristan, an accident had been more likely than a bullet to take a soldier's life.

"We thought it would just drive you nuts, and since we couldn't prove anything—" Delgado turned a dark glare toward Evan. "You told her? After all this time?"

"There's reason to believe the scuttlebutt was right," Megan answered. "I appreciate Evan being straight with me about it and letting me decide what to do."

"You've got new evidence?" Raines looked intrigued.

The quick look Evan gave her underscored her own wariness about giving out too many details. "Just more questions," she said vaguely. "Enough to warrant taking a closer look. You two were with him on that last patrol. Plus Gates, right?"

"Right," Raines agreed.

"Nobody else was there?"

Delgado looked at Raines. "There was that guy from supply, brought us the extra rounds—Merriwether."

"There was another man there?" Evan sounded surprised.

"He wasn't there during the shooting. Just a little bit before," Raines answered.

"Do you know where he is now?"

"Dead," Delgado said bluntly. "Scott Merriwether died in a hit-and-run accident up in north Georgia two months ago."

Chapter Eight

Evan's hand flattened against Megan's back. She tried not to react, but fire danced along her nerve endings where he touched her. "Hit-and-run?"

"Yeah—someone ran him off the road and down a ravine in the Chattahoochee National Forest. Didn't even call 911." Delgado sounded disgusted. "Car caught on fire, and apparently he was trapped inside. Not much left by the time someone finally got to the car."

"I'm sorry to hear that." Megan exchanged a look with Evan. He gave a slight shake of his head—apparently he didn't want to speculate in front of Delgado and Raines. But she had a feeling the subject would come up later—a hit-and-run accident killing one of the witnesses to Vince's shooting?

Too convenient by a long shot.

"What about Gates?" Evan asked. "Where is he now?"

"Last I heard, working in Nashville," Raines answered.

"At Butler Construction," Delgado supplied. "His cousin's the foreman there or something."

Evan removed his hand from Megan's back to type the information into his phone. Cold seeped through to her bones where his hand had been, despite the heat of the day.

"Is there anything else you can tell us? Anything that made you suspect Vince's death wasn't an al Adar attack?" Megan asked. "Besides al Adar being bad shots."

"Vince was spending a lot of his downtime in Tablis," Raines told her. "Which was unusual, 'cause he used to spend all his downtime sending moony letters to you."

Megan frowned, surprised. Vince almost never mentioned trips to the capital in his letters home, until that last one. In fact, he'd said he usually avoided the city during off-duty hours. "A bunch of brass throwing their weight around" was how he'd described Tablis.

"We used to rib him about it—told him we knew he was tryin' to brownnose the brass. Get him one of those Command Sergeant Major buttons on his collar." Delgado's smile faded. "But that wasn't how Sarge did things. I didn't know what he was up to when he'd go to Tablis."

Megan glanced at Evan, wondering what he made of the new information. To her surprise, he showed no sign of surprise.

In fact, he looked guilty.

Had he known about Vince's trips to the capital already? Why hadn't he told her about them?

Raines glanced at his watch and gave Megan an apologetic look. "We're due for a staff meeting in ten minutes. We're going to have to book it to get there. If I think of anything else, I'll email you." He pulled a small spiral notebook from his shirt pocket. "What's your address?"

Megan gave him her email address, then gave him a hug. "Tell Adele I said hello. Give her the email address—I'd love to stay in touch."

Delgado gave her a clumsy hug as he left, too. "Hope you find what you're lookin' for, ma'am."

She fought against a flood of emotion as she watched Vince's men walk out of the mess hall. Evan's hand brushed against her shoulder, making her quiver.

"Anybody else you want to talk to?" he asked quietly.

She turned to look at him. "You knew about Vince's trips to Tablis."

His expression shifted from sympathy to guilt. "Yes."

"You didn't think you needed to mention that to me?"

He looked around the restaurant, which was filling up with a new group of soldiers. "Let's talk about it in the car."

MEGAN KNEW HER WAY AROUND the area better than Evan did, so he let her drive out of the base. She didn't ask any more questions as she navigated them through the checkpoints to leave the base, to Evan's surprise. In fact, once they were back on the highway, it took her another fifty miles of driving before she spoke to him again, snapping the escalating tension filling the air between them.

"Would you like to explain why you didn't mention Vince's trips to Tablis?" she asked, her voice tight with anger.

"I wasn't sure it was relevant," he answered, which was only part of the truth, but he didn't think she'd forgive him for the whole truth. And after the prickly reception he'd received from Delgado and Raines, he had a feeling he'd need Megan's full cooperation to get anything out of Donald Gates.

At least, that was the reason he gave himself. Any other reasons he might have for wanting to stay on Megan Randall's good side weren't relevant, were they? He'd come to Alabama to get the truth about Vince Randall's death, even if the guy had done something to bring it on himself.

Making friends with the widow wasn't part of the plan.

"Not relevant?"

"Lots of soldiers went into Tablis. It was the closest thing to civilization you could find in Kaziristan at the time. There were good restaurants, actual bars with actual drinks—"

"Vince wasn't a drinker. His parents were both alcoholics and he never touched the stuff."

"I don't know why he went to Tablis. Maybe he was looking for a nice anniversary gift for you." He looked at her. "That might be all the package was."

She looked away from the road a second. "You don't really believe that, do you?"

"We'll find Donald Gates and ask about it," he said. "Then we'll worry about what it might mean."

"What about Merriwether's accident? Could it have been something else?"

"Accidents happen. I mean, I didn't even know Merriwether was in the area that night. Hell, I couldn't pick out Scott Merriwether in a lineup. I didn't have much contact with his unit. It's not that likely anyone else would be gunning for him at this late date."

"That's two deaths among the five people there that night."

"And three who are alive," he countered.

Her only response was to look back to the road. He tried to gauge whether or not she was formulating another argument. Her chin was jutting stubbornly, but a quick glance in the rearview mirror later, her expression changed completely, her brow furrowing and her hands tightening on the steering wheel.

Evan looked behind them and spotted a large

black SUV bearing down on them at an alarming rate. "What the hell?"

"Brace yourself," Megan warned, and suddenly the rental car whipped across the road and turned down a crossroad that seemed to head straight into the woods, the movement so fast that his shoulder slammed hard into the passenger door, despite the seat belt holding him in place.

He twisted to look over his shoulder. The SUV had made the same move, though it had lost a little ground.

Megan was gunning the Ford down the narrow two-lane road, the woods flying past them little more than a green blur. "What if this is a dead end?" he asked, gripping the dashboard to keep from pitching forward as she braked into a hairpin turn.

"It's not," she answered tersely, her gaze lifting to the rearview mirror again. She muttered a curse. "When I say brace yourself, I mean it this time." She slammed on the brakes and the Ford fishtailed, tires shrieking on the blacktop. They ended up facing the large black SUV, which was forced to brake before it slammed into them head-on.

As the big vehicle swerved left to miss them, Megan gunned the Ford's engine and bolted past them, heading back up the road in the direction from which they'd come.

"They teach you defensive driving skills at

Homeland Security?" Evan asked, his pulse hammering in his throat.

"No, but it's one of the things we offer at Cooper Security." She whipped the Taurus down an even smaller road that intersected with the side road. Evan darted a quick look behind them during the turn and saw the SUV was still hidden by the sharp curve they'd taken just before the sudden left turn.

Megan peered through the windshield, her eyes narrowed.

"What are you looking for?" he asked.

"There." She pointed to a dirt road turnoff. She slowed into the turn and almost immediately whipped over onto a grassy clearing. She eased the Ford around in the narrow space until the nose pointed toward the road. She cut the engine and jumped out of the car, darting into the woods.

Evan followed her out. "What are we doing?"

"Grab tree branches—big as you can find. For camouflage."

He hoped they'd have time to cover the car before their pursuers figured out where they'd gone. "Just the right and the front," he suggested. "The woods will hide the rest."

They were done in under two minutes. Evan chanced a quick walk to the edge of the dirt road, looking toward the turnoff. No sign of the SUV.

He looked back at the hidden Ford. If he didn't know it was there, it wouldn't be obvious. They might see it if they backtracked, but he was betting they'd go down the road a way first, using the SUV's superior off-road capabilities to catch up to the car on the bumpier unpaved road.

"Do we hide in the car or out?" Megan asked as he returned.

"Outside the car," he decided. If the SUV flew past, then they could run for the car, sweep off the branches and escape the way they'd come. If the SUV came slowly, and spotted the car, the pursuers would take a slow approach, suspecting a trap. That would give him and Megan a head start into the woods.

"Hope you're a good woodswoman," he murmured as he helped her pull their supplies from the Taurus's trunk.

"I'm a Cooper," she said, as if that answered the question.

The sound of a vehicle approaching quickly broke through the muted forest sounds. He caught Megan's arm and pulled her into a crouch behind a large wild hydrangea bush.

Through the trees, he spotted flashes of black as the SUV blasted past their hiding place. Megan started to move as soon as the vehicle was past, but Evan held her in place. "Let me scout first."

He weaved through the woods until he reached the roadside. Risking a quick glance down the road, he spotted the rear end of the SUV as it took a curve with a spray of red dust.

"Go!" he called to Megan, racing to meet her at

the Ford. They ripped the camouflage away, leaving a few smaller twigs that wouldn't budge. The car was already moving as Evan threw himself into the passenger seat and slammed the door behind him.

"How long before they figure out they've been had?" he asked breathlessly, fumbling with the seat belt.

"That road ends in about a mile. So we have maybe a minute or two before they backtrack."

"Then they'll look for us along the road first, right?"

"Maybe." Megan slowed as they reached the side road. "Which way do they expect us to go?"

He thought about it. "Back the way we came."

She nodded and took a right, heading farther down the side road. "This road will take us to I-85 west. We'll take I-85 to I-65 and head north."

"Back to Gossamer Ridge?"

She shook her head. "To Nashville. Somebody doesn't want us to find out what's in that box Vince gave to Donald Gates. So let's find out why it never got to me."

As soon as they felt comfortable that they'd slipped the notice of the black SUV or any other pursuer, Evan told Megan to stop as soon as she could find a place to pull over. She turned off the highway at the next service station they came across and pulled up to the air pump Evan pointed out to her.

"We need air in the tires?" she asked, confused.

Evan reached into the backseat and pulled his briefcase from the floorboard. He dug inside, finally pulling out what looked like a contract. "Well, hell." He slammed the briefcase shut. "The rental company puts GPS trackers on their cars."

"You think that's how they found us?" Megan asked, the sensation of being watched creeping up the back of her neck.

"I doubt it. They must have spotted us leaving Gossamer Ridge and just followed us to Fort Benning. Knowing your history, and since they seem to be pretty sure what we're looking for—in general, at least—"

"It wasn't hard to figure out we'd go to Fort Benning," she finished for him. "But now they have the license plates. If they have any connections to the rental agency at all—"

"We can't risk it. We have to get the tracker off this car," Evan agreed.

"Rental car company isn't going to like it."

"Probably never be allowed to rent a car again." He sighed. "You seem to have a little more experience with GPS trackers—do you think you'd know it if you found it?"

"Depends on how complicated the system." She opened the car door and bent to press the hood latch. "Maybe you should get out and pretend to be putting air in the tires. We don't want to be memorable in case anyone comes by asking questions."

He got out and made a show of checking the tire pressure, while she looked around under the hood. She spotted a small box on the inside of the Taurus's right front fender.

"Cooper Security will cover your expenses," she said as she surreptitiously dropped the tracker in the nearby garbage bin. "Let's fill up and go."

Within an hour and a half, they were passing through Birmingham. Megan started looking for an exit with a good selection of fast-food places, ending up in a northern suburb, where they made a quick bathroom stop at a hamburger joint and got their food to go.

Walking back to the car, Megan felt delayed reaction beginning to set in. Her limbs were shaky.

"Are you good to drive for a while?" she asked Evan.

He nodded, his eyes narrowing. "Are you okay?"

"Just starting to get tired. Long, stressful few hours."

"Maybe we should head back to Chickasaw County instead. Get a full night's sleep and start fresh in the morning."

She shook her head. "I want to reach Nashville before nightfall. Scope out where Donald Gates is living now and work out how we plan to approach him." Her cell phone vibrated in her purse, interrupting her train of thought. She checked the display. It was her brother Jesse. "Hey. What's up?"

"I could ask the same of you," Jesse drawled flatly. "You promised to call and check in."

"I was a little busy." She glanced at Evan, wondering how much she should tell her brother about their encounter with the SUV. Evan's poker face didn't offer any advice, so she decided to go with a variation of the truth. "We thought we were being followed for a while, so we changed routes. We've got a lead on who might know something about the missing package, so we're heading there this afternoon."

"Heading where?"

"Nashville," she answered. "And I need you to get me an address from this phone number." She read Donald Gates's cell phone number to him.

"I'll call you back in a few." Jesse hung up.

Megan looked at Evan, who was watching her with a look of bemusement.

"'Thought someone was following us'?"

"Trust me, we don't need the Cooper Cavalry rushing to the rescue right now."

"Except when you need an address or a posse."

She couldn't argue with that.

"You're lucky to have them watching your back," he said, a faint tone of envy in his voice. She wondered if he was thinking about the brother he lost.

"I know. I guess I take it for granted that I have a great family around to cover my tail." She shouldn't complain so much. Without her family, she wasn't sure she'd have been able to get through the past four years without losing her mind.

At the car, Evan slid behind the wheel, while Megan settled into the passenger seat, kicking off her sandals and tucking her feet up under her on the seat. Buckling up, she turned to look at Evan. "Is this turning out the way you thought it would?"

"Coming to Alabama? Or my investigation of Vince's death?"

"Either. Both."

"I don't know if I had any expectations," he said carefully. "I'd hit so many walls already."

"How long have you been looking into it?" she asked, surprised she'd never thought to ask him that question before.

"Going on two years."

She stared. "And it took you this long to come to me?"

He glanced away from the road long enough to meet her questioning gaze. "At first, it was just the vaguest of questions. A faint suspicion something was wrong with the official story."

"And you already felt guilty."

His gaze tangled with hers again for a second. "Yes."

"If that's what's driving you—"

"It's part of it, but not all of it," he said firmly. "Not even most of it. Not anymore."

"Good. Because then I'd have to feel guilty, and

who needs that?" She smiled, but her humor faded quickly. "Even if it wasn't the SSU who shot Vince, I'm certain it wasn't al Adar. Nobody sends goons to cover up a war casualty."

Her phone rang minutes later. It was Jesse with an address. She jotted it down. "Thanks. Got it. Now, one more favor? There's a death I want you to look into." She told him about the hit-and-run crash that had killed Merriwether.

"You don't think it's an accident?"

"That's what I need to find out."

"I'll look into it." His voice darkened with warning. "You be careful, okay?"

"I will." She hung up and turned to Evan. "He worries."

Evan's brow wrinkled as he pulled onto the interstate. "So do I."

By the time they reached Nashville, they'd made three fruitless attempts to reach Donald Gates on the phone. He didn't seem to have an answering machine or service, either.

"What do you think?" Megan asked, turning to look at Evan as they stopped at a traffic light near the Ryman Theater. "Find somewhere to stay tonight and try to call Gates tomorrow? Or go see him tonight?"

"Let's go see him. Get it over with."

The address Jesse had given them turned out to be a modest bungalow-style house in the McFerrin Park neighborhood. It was an older home, a little on the shabby side compared to some in the area, and rental signs scattered through the yards of nearby houses suggested Gates might be renting, as well. Megan hoped he hadn't moved already without leaving a forwarding address.

In the waning afternoon light, the house lay quiet and dark. Megan checked her watch and saw it was after six. Was he working late? Or had he gone out for drinks after work?

She climbed the shallow steps to the front stoop and knocked on the door. It moved the second her knuckles touched it, swinging open with an eerie creak.

Almost immediately, a sickly smell wafted onto the stoop from inside. Megan's gut twisted into a knot.

Next to her, Evan growled a low profanity. He, too, knew immediately what the odor meant.

Someone inside the house was already very dead.

Chapter Nine

When Evan had been a little boy, he'd stumbled onto a body in the woods behind his house. Drug overdose, as it turned out. The man had been lying out in the elements for at least a week. It had taken second and third looks for Evan to figure out what he was seeing, but he'd known from the smell that whatever lay in the underbrush was long dead.

He could still remember the smell.

Donald Gates hadn't been dead quite that long. Over twenty-four hours, almost certainly, based on the smell of decay, but he was still in the early stages of decomposition. Still recognizable, despite the discoloration from the onset of cyanosis. He'd been shot—chest and leg. The leg shot he could have survived, at Evan's best guess.

The chest shot was straight through the heart.

Evan stood still for a moment, listening. It wasn't likely that the person who'd shot Gates was hanging around after so many hours. But he waited through a minute of silent stillness before he backed away from the kitchen, avoiding the blood and other fluids that had leaked from the body and pooled on the floor underneath. "We need to call the cops."

Megan stood in the doorway with her hand over her nose and mouth, her sickened gaze fixed on the body moldering on the linoleum floor. She moved her hand away long enough to ask, "Is it Gates?"

"Yeah."

"We can't call the police yet." She squared her shoulders. "We have to look around to see if he still has the package Vince gave him to send to me."

"You're talking about disturbing a crime scene—"

"This could be my only chance to find it!" She turned to him with desperate eyes. "I won't disturb anything—"

"The police will find your fingerprints—"

"I have latex gloves in the first-aid kit I packed."

He stared at her, realizing she wouldn't be deterred. "Fiber and hair evidence—"

"I'm looking around for other possible victims."

He met her challenging stare, torn between doing what he had been taught was the right thing to do—and what he knew, gut deep, was the only thing they could do.

If the police found the package, they'd take it in for evidence, and it might be months before Megan was allowed to have whatever lay inside.

Assuming the package was here in the first place. Or that the killers had left anything to find.

"Okay," he said finally. "But in ten minutes, we're calling the police."

They covered the small house methodically, each taking different rooms. About five minutes into the search, Evan heard Megan call his name from a small spare bedroom in the back. He hurried down the hall and found her standing over a brown cardboard box that lay on the floor of an open closet. She was gazing at the box as if she'd just found the Holy Grail.

"It could be just a box," he warned.

"Read what's written on the side." She pointed.

He walked around until he could see the boldly inked block letters that read "PATTON."

"Vince wrote that," she said with conviction. "Do you have a pen on you?"

As he handed her the pen, he saw that the box top had already been untaped and opened. There might be nothing left inside at all.

Or it might be booby-trapped, he realized just as she bent to push the pen under the flaps to open it.

"Wait—"

But she'd already tipped up the flap. Inside, nothing sprang out or exploded, and Evan exhaled, bending closer to see what was inside.

It was a stuffed toy, a blue fox with bright gold eyes, about the size of a squirrel. Megan reached into the box and pulled it out, holding it up, her eyes bright with tears.

"It was a toy for Patton," she said softly, meeting his gaze with a disconcerting mixture of delight and despair.

Evan stared at the plush toy, feeling flattened. This was what Vince Randall had sent home to his wife? A toy?

Some smoking gun.

"I'm taking this home with me," she said flatly, in a tone that invited no argument. "It has nothing to do with why Gates was killed."

"It's probably exactly why he was killed," Evan disagreed.

"It won't tell the police a thing," she said in a tone that reminded him of a cat's growl. "It's the last thing Vince sent me, Evan. And for whatever reason, Gates kept it from me."

And if the cops took it as evidence, it would be ages before they gave it back to her.

"Okay. But don't let anyone see you take it outside."

She pulled up the hem of her T-shirt, revealing a flat, toned stomach that might have sparked some very masculine fantasies if Evan weren't standing in a house that smelled like days-old death. She slipped the toy into the waistband of her pants, under her arm, and dropped the shirt hem down again, effectively hiding the toy.

She headed quickly to the front door. Evan followed, emerging into the afternoon heat with palpable relief. He breathed deeply, letting the fresh air fill his nose and lungs, and longed for a shower to wash away the lingering smell of death that seemed to permeate his clothes and skin.

Megan went to the car and sat in the passenger seat, bending out of view. She sat up again and re-emerged from the car, returning to where he stood on the walkway, dialing 911. "I put the toy in my bag and also put my Ruger in its case. You may want to do the same with your Kel-Tec."

Good point, he conceded. His North Carolina CCW—license to carry a concealed weapon— was honored in Tennessee just as it was in Alabama, but having a weapon on him when the police arrived to investigate a gun homicide would be downright stupid.

He finished giving the dispatcher the location of Gates's house and went to the car to stow away his weapon.

The Nashville police cruiser arrived about ten minutes later, lights and sirens off, since Evan had made it clear to the dispatcher that the victim had been dead for a while. One patrolman stayed outside with Megan and Evan while the other took a look around inside. The one inside returned, grimacing, and called for the crime-scene investigators.

While waiting for the evidence technicians, one of the officers asked them what their business was in the area.

The other officer drew Evan away, effectively separating him from Megan. It was common practice, separating the witnesses so they couldn't get their stories straight, he knew.

Of course, he and Megan had had ten minutes of waiting to get their story straight already. "Private Gates was in the army with Mrs. Randall's late husband," Evan told the officer. "She wanted to talk to him about her husband's last hours—Private Gates was on patrol with him when he died."

"And what's your connection?"

"I worked as a Pentagon liaison with Sergeant Randall's unit when he died. I helped her track down Private Gates."

It was the truth, if an incomplete version, unencumbered by the slowly unfolding conspiracy of silence his investigation had begun to uncover. Raising those allegations now would do little to solve Donald Gates's murder. But they would almost certainly complicate things for Evan and Megan, perhaps even force them to stay in town overnight, undergoing further questioning.

Evan didn't think Megan could take much more today. She'd held together well enough inside Gates's house, focused on the mystery she'd come to Nashville to solve. But the disappointing outcome, and the stresses of the last two days, had begun to take a visible toll.

Her face, fair to begin with, had taken on a pasty pallor that made her freckles stand out in bright relief. Dark circles bruised the skin beneath her eyes, and her shoulders slumped as the officer walked away and joined his partner on the front stoop of Gates's house.

Detectives arrived within a half hour, a tall, broad-shouldered black man in his forties and a younger, thinner white man in his mid-thirties. The older man wore a suit that looked as if it was about to melt into his skin under the heat of the Nashville afternoon, but the younger detective had shrugged off his jacket and was in shirtsleeves rolled up to his elbows. While the uniformed officers waited outside with Evan and Megan, the detectives took a look inside.

They returned a few minutes later, separated Megan and Evan again, and the interviews repeated. Yes, Evan told the detective, he and Megan had gone inside the residence. They smelled decay and wanted to know if their friend was hurt or worse. Yes, they'd gone in other rooms, looking for other possible victims. No, they didn't know who would have done such a thing. Yes, they had alibis for the last forty-eight to seventy-two hours.

It didn't take long for the detectives to ascertain—with a series of calls to Alabama—that Megan and Evan could account for their whereabouts for the previous two days, putting them over a hundred miles away when Donald Gates had been murdered.

"I'm going to type up your statement later. Can you come by and sign them?" the younger detective asked.

"We were heading back to Alabama tonight," Evan said. "Can you send the statements to law enforcement in Alabama so we can sign them there?"

The detective looked reluctant but agreed, though he insisted on getting phone numbers where he could reach them if he had any more questions.

By seven that evening, they were on the road again. From the looks of Megan's pinched, wan face, she felt as wrung-out as he did. The thought of sinking into the big, soft bed at his Gossamer Mountain cabin was the only thing keeping him going.

"How'd the intruders know about the package?" Megan asked.

"I don't know," Evan admitted. "They killed Donald long before we even knew the package existed."

Her voice darkened. "He was shot straight through the heart, wasn't he?"

Evan nodded. Just like Vince Randall. Probably a handgun instead of the rifle that killed Vince, almost certainly fitted with a sound suppressor. An SSU special, it seemed.

"It's the SSU, don't you think?" Megan asked aloud, echoing his silent thoughts.

"Yes."

"They shot him in the leg first—to get him to talk." He could tell she was trying to remain focused and unemotional, but strain tinted her voice. "Did they shoot him for this?"

He looked at her and saw she was holding the blue fox in clenched hands.

"There's no way to know that," he said quietly. It wasn't a lie to placate her; he really didn't know why they'd gone after Donald Gates. "It could be entirely unrelated. We don't know what kind of life he'd been living since he left the army."

"What about Merriwether?"

"Your brother's looking into that. Until we discover evidence to the contrary, maybe we should assume it was an accident, just as it was ruled."

She turned her weary eyes toward him. "I want to go home. I want to get my dog, give him Vince's gift and forget any of this happened. Can we do that?"

"Of course," he answered, heading the car onto the I-65 South onramp. Next to him, Megan closed her eyes and curled her fingers around the blue fox, looking tired and defeated.

He couldn't blame her. He felt pretty beaten himself.

THEY MADE IT BACK to Gossamer Ridge by ten-thirty that evening. To Megan's surprise, Evan insisted on following her to Isabel's to pick up Patton, then stayed with her all the way back to her house. He parked behind her Jeep and walked with her and the excited mutt up to the porch.

He bent close, as if he were about to kiss her. Her heart skipped a beat and heat flooded her cheeks.

"The bugs are still going, right?" he whispered.

Her heart stuttered again. She'd forgotten about the listening devices. "I think so," she whispered back.

"Maybe we should let them know we found nothing." As he pulled back, his stubbled jaw brushed against hers. She'd always loved the pleasure-pain of Vince's beard rasping against her skin, a reminder of his masculinity, of the unmistakable, wonderful differences between men and women. Desire flooded her, fierce and unexpected.

But not unwelcome, she realized. Not unwanted.

She felt a little breathless as she pulled out her keys and unlocked the front door. Inside, the place looked undisturbed. Patton strained against his leash and she reached down to unhook his collar, letting him go.

She locked gazes with Evan, nearly melting under the smoldering heat of his regard.

"You glad to be home, boy?" His gaze never faltered.

"I know I am," she said, her voice raspy. "That trip was a big bust. Can't believe we wasted all that time."

"I'm sorry. I feel I led you on a wild-goose chase."

"Yeah, well. We know something's up, with all those people chasing after us."

"I was so sure we'd find that package."

His words reminded her of the blue fox plush toy in her bag. She unzipped the side pocket and pulled out the toy. Patton wagged his tail wildly and grinned at her in giddy anticipation. She gave the toy to the dog and he ran around the room in delight.

Her heart hurt a little that Vince never got to see him enjoy the fox. Not that the toy would have lasted that long anyway—Patton was already chewing off the plastic eyes and digging out the stuffing.

"Why did they kill Donald Gates if there wasn't a package?" she asked aloud, looking up at Evan. "That doesn't make sense, does it?"

"I'm beginning to think none of my theories make sense anymore." Evan made a face that made her smile. "I guess I need to go back to square one."

"Where is square one? The Pentagon?"

"Maybe. Or maybe I'll just stop beating my head against a wall and go back home to North Carolina."

She realized this wasn't part of his playacting. He really thought it was time for him to go home. Her stomach knotted. "When?"

"Maybe as soon as tomorrow."

A storm of emotions rocked her, made her want to move, to run, to do something to release the restless energy clawing at her chest. She didn't know if she felt heartbroken or relieved, excited or terrified.

The only emotion she could identify with any

certainty was the one burning in her chest like a bonfire.

Pure, raw desire.

Evan Pike was about to walk out of her life, and she wasn't ready for it. She wanted him to stay.

The burning ache in her chest propelled her forward until she crashed into him, body to body. His eyes widening, he put his arms out to catch her, and his hand brushed the side of her breast. She sucked in a gasp.

His eyes darkened to embers, heat flaring in their depths. Slowly, he ran his hand down the curve of her waist, part caress, part exploration. He lifted his other hand to her shoulder, his thumb sliding along the contour of her collarbone.

He bent his head slowly, deliberately, his cheek brushing against hers. "Is this for show?" he whispered.

She drew back and looked up at him, her heart pounding with fear. What was she doing? "I don't know what it is," she whispered back.

He cupped her face between his large hands, his thumbs moving across the tracks of the tears she didn't realize had spilled down her cheeks. "You're a beautiful woman." He said it aloud, where any of the listening devices could easily pick it up. "I want you."

She felt helpless against the onslaught of desire sparked by his soft declaration. Helpless against the answering fire that burned out of control. Still clutching the pages of Vince's letter in her fist, she rose on her toes and wrapped her arms around his neck, driving him against the front door.

His arms snaked around her waist, pulling her closer. He gazed at her for a long moment, so long she felt as if she would combust. Then he dipped his head to kiss her, his mouth hot and soft and darkly sweet, like sugarcane.

Her lips trembled apart, surrendering to the only thing in this upturned, maddened world that made sense. The universe spun around her, a kaleidoscope of exquisite sensations that made her lungs burn and her knees shake.

Across the room, Patton made a playful growling sound, low in his throat, the sound seeping into the heated fog swirling around her brain. She dragged her mouth away from Evan's and looked over at Patton. He was lying on his stomach, the mangled blue fox between his paws. He picked up the toy in his mouth and gave it a violent shake.

A cylindrical piece of metal flew out of the toy's ripped belly and rolled across the floor toward Megan. She stopped it with her shoe and picked it up, staring.

It was a large shell casing—maybe as large as a .50 caliber. There was no bullet inside, but what looked like tightly rolled pieces of paper had been stuffed into the shell.

She showed it to Evan. His eyes widened.

She tried to pry the papers out with her fingertip but couldn't get any leverage.

Evan pulled a multi-blade knife from his back pocket and handed it over. He bent close, his jaw rasping along her cheek again as he whispered in her ear. "There's a small set of tweezers tucked into the knife casing."

"I'm going to be sad to see you go," she said aloud as she found the tweezers and grabbed one of the sheets of paper. Clamping hard, she pulled it free. Four pieces of rolled-up paper came out. She saw they were covered with tiny writing.

Unmistakably Vince's handwriting.

She scanned the pages that had writing on both sides of the paper. She found what appeared to be the first page of the missive and read it silently.

Darling Meggie, if Patton's the pup I remember, you probably found this five minutes after you gave him the toy.

She smiled, even as tears welled up in her eyes. She thumbed them away and kept reading.

I'm sending this information in the toy because I'm afraid the brass is looking at all the mail going out. These pages contain everything I know about what's going on in Tablis,

Kaziristan. I know some of it won't make sense, but I hope to make it home soon to explain everything—

Her vision blurred again. She blinked hard and read on.

Keep this information safe. It could bring down a lot of people in high places.

She looked up. Evan's expression was one part fierce curiosity, one part gentle sympathy.

He bent his forehead to hers, his breath rapid and hot. "Let's get out of here," he whispered. "Get Patton. I'll get your bag."

Shoving the roll of papers into her pocket, she did as he said, her hands trembling as she attached the leash to Patton's collar. She gave him the empty cloth shell of the blue fox and he carried it happily in his mouth all the way to Evan's car.

Evan put Patton in the back while Megan got into the passenger seat. He came around the car and slid behind the wheel, turning to look at her briefly before his gaze dropped to the papers in her hand. "Is that what I think it is?"

She nodded. "This is what they didn't want us to find."

Chapter Ten

"Isabel and Ben are at a late movie in Borland," Megan told Evan as she closed her phone, "but she said we can leave Patton in the backyard and they'll take care of him until I can come get him again."

"You have a very understanding family," he murmured, distracted by the way his whole body still tingled from her kiss. He didn't know what had caused her sudden overture—didn't care, really. As long as they got to do it again.

Soon.

He followed her directions back to Ben and Isabel's house, the road still unfamiliar and that much harder to navigate in the dark. They put Patton and his new toy in the backyard, left the leash on the front porch and returned to the car.

"The cabin?" he asked.

"For now," she agreed, pulling the pages out of her pocket. She flicked on the sun visor light and peered at the tiny writing. "Most of this seems to be notes more than a letter," she said. "He didn't write out everything." Frustration lined her brow. "I guess he planned to be here to interpret."

Her melancholy tone made his chest hurt. "He should've been here."

Her chin shot up. "But he's not. So it's up to us."

He liked that she seemed to be including him in the mission. Not just because his guilty conscience made him want to be there for her, but also because he liked being part of a team again. And if half the team was a leggy, beautiful mess of a woman who intrigued him like no one he'd ever met before— well, he'd just have to deal with it.

The cabin lay still and stately in the moonlight. He parked on the gravel drive and cut the engine, watching the silent facade with wary tension.

"I don't see any movement," Megan murmured.

"Still, let's leave our bags in the car until we take a look around inside."

"In case we need to make a run for it?" Her voice was low and bone dry.

"Exactly." He opened the car door. The loud creak of the hinges made him cringe. The slam of the door was worse. He knew he was being paranoid, expecting an ambush around every corner or behind every bush.

Even though he stepped slowly up the porch steps, his boots thudded audibly on the wood planks. With a soft exhalation, he bent and pulled the Kel-Tec from his ankle holster.

It was a strange feeling, this primal instinct to

pull out a weapon before he entered a place. But that's what his life had become, long before his trip to Gossamer Ridge. And the escalating threats against him—and now, Megan—had only honed the instinct to a razor's edge.

Beside him, a glint caught his eye. He glanced sideways and saw that Megan had already unsheathed her Ruger, ready to cover his back. She shot him a wry look and nodded at the door.

He carefully turned the key in the lock and pushed it open. Nothing detonated. No sounds from within suggested an intruder lay in wait. Staying on the porch, he reached inside and flicked the switch. Light flooded the cabin's spacious front room, illuminating furniture and decor but no bad guys lurking to take him or Megan down with a few well-aimed shots.

Still, they moved together in unspoken unison, room to room, looking for any signs that someone had been here while they were gone.

There was nothing. The place remained undisturbed.

They finished their circuit in the great room again. Evan put away his gun and turned to Megan. "Why haven't they found this place yet?"

"Maybe they didn't know to check your GPS unit after all."

"But they know I'm working with you." He waved his hand at the cabin. "And this is definitely Cooper territory."

She shook her head. "Maybe they just haven't yet connected you to the Gossamer Lake Coopers yet. Not all cousins are as close as we are."

"They seem ready to come to your aid in a heartbeat."

"Their mom practically raised us kids. Aunt Beth was a trained nurse, just like our mom. I think that's how my parents met, through Aunt Beth." Megan's smile held a hint of melancholy. "We skinned a knee, we ran to Aunt Beth like she was our mom. We took family vacations with our cousins, too. Both sets."

"Both sets?"

"My dad has two brothers—Uncle Mike and Uncle Jay. Uncle Mike has seven kids. Uncle Jay has eight."

That was a lot of first cousins, even for a Southern family. "You Coopers must be a fertile bunch."

She grinned. "Seems that way. Three of Uncle Jay's kids are adopted, though. So the Cooper fertility genes can only account for five."

He had cousins all over Kentucky, mostly on his mother's side. She had been a girl from the eastern hills, whose family had lived in the mountains and hollows for generations. But he barely knew any of them anymore. Hadn't seen them in years, not since he rode a bus out of Cumberland and never looked back.

"What are you thinking about?" Megan asked, apprehension coloring her raspy alto.

Noting the dark smudges beneath her eyes and the weary lines on her face, he wished he'd never brought her into this mess. If there had been a way to keep her clear—

But there hadn't. He'd already gotten farther in two days working with her than he'd managed in two years. "I'm thinking it's late and we've had a wretched day," he said aloud.

Her brow creased. "That's not all you were thinking."

"I was also thinking I should be sorry I kissed you," he added honestly. "But I'm not."

Her lips quirked. "You didn't do it by yourself."

Her lopsided smile sent heat jolting through him. "You know I want to kiss you right now, don't you?"

"I reckon I do."

He cupped her cheek in his palm, brushing his thumb across her lower lip. "So many really good reasons why we shouldn't."

She sighed and backed away. "Startin' with this." She reached into the pocket of her jeans and pulled out the rolled-up sheets of paper she'd found inside the dog toy.

"Why don't we try to get some sleep before we worry about this?" he suggested. "It'll be here in the morning."

"Can't sleep," she admitted. "But you go on to bed." She crossed to the sofa and pulled the coffee table closer.

He slid in next to her, covering her hands as she unrolled the papers. "Megan, don't drive yourself until you're sick. Vince wouldn't want that. *I* don't want that."

Her hands trembled in his. "We're already so far behind."

He drew her around to face him. "I don't know why Gates didn't send the toy to you. Even if he was crooked, if he was in on it with the SSU, once he opened the package and saw it was just a toy, I don't get why he didn't send it then."

"And now we can't ask him."

He stroked the tumble of red curls away from her forehead. "I know you want answers, but nobody said you had to be the one to find them. I'm in this until the end—I'll do it for you. Give me Vince's notes and let me handle it. You just go back home to your family and be safe—"

The look she gave him made his stomach hurt. "Everybody tries to protect me, Evan, and I'm tired of it. I have to do this myself." Her voice rose. "I have to feel it all, make it real, because the easiest thing in the world would be to pretend Vince was still alive somewhere, and any day now, he'll come home. The pain keeps me sane. It keeps me tied to reality."

He caught her flailing hand, pulled her palm flat against his chest. He wondered if she could feel the rapid cadence of his heart beneath. "So you have to read those notes yourself."

She nodded. "He sent them to me. I'm the one who was supposed to see them."

He let go of her hand. "You don't want me to see them."

"I just want to see them first. Alone." She touched his chest again, her fingers warm. "Please understand."

A shiver skated up his spine as a new thought occurred to him. Did she suspect the same thing about her husband that he did? Did she fear what Vince Randall may have confessed in those notes, what complicity he might have had in the conspiracy that had taken his life?

Would she try to hide her husband's sins?

He'd have to take that risk. Because she was right—Vince had sent the letter to her. He'd trusted her with whatever information he'd included in his notes.

Evan would have to trust her, too.

"I'll go get our bags," he said.

THE THIRD TIME THROUGH VINCE'S letter, Megan realized she couldn't decipher everything on her own. When Vince had written these notes, he had expected to be coming home within a few months. His tour of duty had been nearly done, with no signs that the army was going to extend the tour for his unit. In fact, they'd come home right on time.

Vince just hadn't been with them.

Too much of what she was reading was Vince's

shorthand, and she had a feeling that someone who'd been there with him in Kaziristan could make more sense of the abbreviations and acronyms. But Evan had gone to bed over an hour ago. Shouldn't she just try again in the morning when he was with her?

The sound of a door opening made her jump, reminding her just how long a day she'd already had. She turned to find Evan in the open doorway of his bedroom, leaning against the door frame. He wore black running shorts and a white tank top that hugged his lean, muscular torso like a lover. A tingle of female appreciation shot through her, head to toe.

"Couldn't sleep," he said, watching her from the doorway. He nodded toward the pages. "Anything new?"

"I don't know," she confessed. "I think so, but it's like reading Greek. And I don't speak Greek."

He walked toward her with a loose-limbed gait that sent awareness jolting through her. As he bent over her shoulder to look at the pages, his masculine scent filled her lungs, a potent combination of soap and something raw-edged and darkly masculine.

"What do we have?" He sounded focused but tired, and she thought she heard a hint of a Southern drawl trying to creep into his neutral accent. Maybe being down here was starting to rub off on him.

"The gist of what I've learned is that Vince had gotten wind of some hinky goings-on between some of the MacLear security forces and al Adar. He uses 'aA" here, but that's how he used to abbreviate al Adar in his letters home. He thought there was a middleman, someone Vince referenced as SDBR."

"State Department's Barton Reid?" Evan guessed, his breath kissing her cheek.

She glanced up and found him leaning so close that her forehead brushed against his cheek when she moved. He returned her gaze, his eyes dark with arousal.

She turned her head away, flooded by desire so potent it made her dizzy. "That's what I was thinking." She cleared her throat. "Vince says he tried to talk to his brigade leader about what he'd seen, but 'SDBR' was in his C.O.'s tent when he arrived, in some sort of—what's BSCJ?"

Evan chuckled, the sound rumbling through her like summer thunder. "Big-shot circle—well, you can guess the rest."

That made sense. If Vince had found his commanding officer meeting with Barton Reid, then he might have come to believe the contact between Reid and the known terrorist target was sanctioned by people much higher up the government food chain. "If Vince thought the government was involved in secret talks with the terrorists who'd been shooting at him and his men, I don't think he would just turn a blind eye and trust that they know what they're doing."

"I don't think we *were* negotiating with terrorists." Evan pulled up a spare chair to the table where she sat. He scooted it closer to her and sat, giving her a thoughtful look. "I wish I'd known about Vince's suspicions. I wish he'd told me. It could have changed everything."

"Like what?"

"I would have come to you sooner, for one thing."

"Sooner than now?"

"I put it off—" He pressed his lips to a thin line. "I thought Vince might have been involved."

It took a second to realize what he meant. "You thought Vince was working with the SSU?"

"I couldn't explain the sudden frequency of his trips to Tablis. And—" He paused, clearly reluctant.

"And what?" she prodded.

"Innocent people don't get shot nearly as often as people who are doing things they're not supposed to."

Anger rose like fever in her cheeks. "You thought Vince brought his own death on himself?"

Before Evan could answer, a soft rattle above them brought them both to startled attention. Evan laid his hand on her arm as if to warn her to be quiet as he rose and moved toward the center of the room, his gaze directed upward.

"Animal?" he asked.

The noise came again. Muted. Furtive.

Definitely not an animal.

She shook her head and slid her Ruger from the holster still clipped to her jeans. Joining him where he stood, she spoke in a whisper. "Roof? Or attic?"

"Attic."

"You need to be dressed to run. Now." She bent and picked up her still-packed bag from where it lay by the sofa.

He wrapped his arm around her shoulders. "We don't get split up—agreed?"

She nodded.

His arm still around her, he led her to his bedroom. He hadn't unpacked much, either. His bag lay open but mostly full, as if he'd anticipated having to make another run for it. "They'll have disabled the car so we can't get away easily."

She hadn't thought of that. "My cousin Gabe lives just down the mountain. He can lend us his boat and we can cross the lake to my brother Wade's place. He has a truck we can use."

He slipped a pair of black jeans over his shorts and quickly swapped out a black T-shirt for the white tank. Overhead, more furtive noises drove them to move faster. While she finished throwing clothes into his bag, he pulled a large black SIG Sauer P220 out of a hard-shell case and quickly loaded a clip of .45 ammunition. He fished a shoulder holster from his bag and strapped it in place. The Kel-Tec P32 in his ankle holster went on last.

"What do you think they're waiting for?" she asked, realizing she was clutching the roll of pages in her fist so tightly her fingernails were digging into her palm.

"Maybe they're hoping we'll go to bed," he murmured. "Better to catch us while we're completely vulnerable. But I'm not sure how much longer they'll wait."

"How do we get out of here? They could have the place surrounded."

"I'm sure they do," he conceded, looking grim.

"I can call my family," she suggested. "Lots of backup."

"That just sets up a hostage situation," he said. "We're going to have to figure a way out ourselves."

"The last time the SSU came after a Cooper up here, they were lured into a trap. I'm not sure they'll make the same mistake twice," she warned.

"We need to know what we're up against," he said. "Any idea how much space is in the attic? That could tell us how many people are inside right now."

"Hold on." Megan fished her cell phone from her pocket and dialed her cousin Hannah's number. Hannah answered on the third ring, sounding groggy.

Megan filled her cousin in on their dilemma, keeping her voice low and her words terse. "How big is the attic? How many people could it hold?"

"Not many—three, tops, and it'd be cramped. There's a big attic fan—we encourage people to use it during the milder months instead of the air conditioners—"

"Like the one that Aunt Sandy and Uncle Jay used to have?"

"Almost exactly," Hannah confirmed.

Megan glanced at Evan, who was watching her with curiosity. "Where's the switch?" she asked Hannah.

"In the master bedroom closet." Hannah's tone changed. "Oh, Megs, that's bloody brilliant."

"Let's hope it is." She wasn't sure what would happen next, but it would at least stir their intruders into enough action to reveal their presence.

"What about backup?"

"Send out the alarm," Megan said quickly. "But tell them to be careful. It could easily turn into a siege situation with hostages." She looked up at Evan. "Us."

After she hung up, she crossed quietly to the closet and eased the door open. Inside, she saw the oversize switch that would turn on the enormous fan in the attic.

"You're going to turn on the fan?"

She nodded. "Ought to stir up a little action up there, don't you think?"

"Then what?"

"Backup's coming—if we can hold 'em off—"

"No, wait." Evan shut off the bedroom light,

plunging the room into darkness. Megan *felt* more than *saw* his movement across the room to the windows, which were covered by lined curtains designed to block light from outside. He inched one curtain aside, letting in a sliver of pale moonlight. "Will these windows open or are they painted shut?"

"I'm not sure," she admitted, moving to stand by him.

"Let's hope they will," he said. "We'll have just one chance to make this work." He stepped closer, the warmth of his body enveloping her, giving her a strange sense of calm. As if whatever they were facing could be conquered as long as they stuck together. She hadn't felt that sensation with anyone else since Vince's death, not even her family.

"I see movement," he whispered.

She looked through the narrow opening. A dark figure darted through the woods, edging closer to the house. A second moved into position nearby.

"We need a distraction—something to draw them around to the front," Evan said, his voice tense with sudden excitement. "Ever made any firecrackers from scratch?"

She grinned up at him, already reaching for her Ruger. "Matter of fact, I have."

Within five minutes, they'd pried open five bullet casings and emptied out the black powder inside. Using some clear plastic tape Megan found in the kitchen drawer, they built thirty small fire-crackers, using pieces of string as fuses.

"Tape them together in three sets of ten," Megan suggested. "We can put a longer fuse on one in each set and soak it with lighter fluid. I think I saw some in the kitchen when I was looking for the string."

"Good idea," Evan said approvingly. "We'll put one string on the back porch, one on the side porch and leave one popping in the front room."

"Put them in pans—make 'em rattle even more." She was grinning, despite the fear. Nothing more satisfying than doing something—anything—to get yourself out of a mess.

"If they decide to come down and check on what we're up to, this could all be for nothing," Evan warned as he weaved the longer fuse through the string of firecrackers.

"We probably need to make more normal sound-ing noise. Run the shower, maybe. Turn on a tele-vision."

"Good idea. Stay right here." Evan disappeared for a moment across the short hallway into the room with the bunk beds. The television came on, the volume low but easily audible. One of the late-night talk shows she never watched. He came back into the darkened bedroom. "That ought to give them a little pause," he said.

"I think we have to hide what we're doing," she said. She'd given their plan a little thought while they were making the firecrackers. "Maybe you can go on the back porch and make a lot of noise. Turn on the hot tub, pretend you're going to take a soak?"

He looked down at her, his eyes gleaming in the light seeping into the room from the television in the other bedroom. "I think they'd find you more distracting in a hot tub than me."

"Well, since neither of us is actually going to get into the hot tub, you do it. I'll put the second string on the side porch, then text your phone from the front room and we'll light them all at once. Then we run to the bedroom and when the first firecracker goes off, I'll turn on the attic fan and scramble the guys upstairs. Sound like a plan?"

"If the guys guarding the window don't make a move toward the other side of the house, we may have to take them on ourselves," Evan warned. "Are you ready for that?"

She'd never killed a human being before. But she'd been hunting a time or two. She was good with a Ruger, and if they could take out one or both of the outside guards, she could probably do some damage with one of those rifles they were carrying around. She raised her chin. "I'm ready."

Evan grabbed a towel from the master bath— for his hot tub cover—and they headed to the dark kitchen for the rest of their supplies. Feeling around the cabinets, Megan found some shallow metal baking pans to hold the firecrackers. She took two and gave one to Evan. He slipped the pan, the kitchen match and flint, and his firecrackers under the towel.

She started to move away from him, toward the front room, but Evan stopped her, his fingers warm and firm as they closed around her arm. Turning her to face him, he whispered, "Good luck."

She gazed up at his dark shape in the shadows of the kitchen. "You, too."

He bent his head toward her, catching her by surprise. His lips covered hers, hot and sweet and maddening. Clutching the pans and the firecrackers more tightly to her chest, she kissed him back until the creeping madness threatened to derail their plan entirely. She pulled away, fighting the shakiness taking hold in her arms and legs. "I'll text you when I'm ready."

As she hurried to the side porch, she heard the back door open. Evan was going outside, making a show of starting the hot tub. She heard the water turn on and eased the side porch door open, sliding the pan through. She left it open a crack and hurried to the fireplace for the lighter. She put the firecrackers in the pan and thumbed on the lighter. It made a soft hiss and filled the area in front of the door with a soft, golden aura. She pulled her cell phone out, typed in Evan's number and the message Go.

Then she touched the flame to the fuse.

Chapter Eleven

Bending over the pan of homemade firecrackers, Evan lit the long matchstick. With a hiss, it flared, lighting up the dark porch for a second. He took a deep breath, touched the flame to the fuse and dashed out of the kitchen.

He nearly ran into Megan as she bolted toward the bedroom. He caught her as she stumbled, pressing his nose into her wild curls, breathing in the warm herbal tang of her shampoo. It had become a familiar scent, he realized, a part of the fabric of his existence over the past two days.

He parted from her with reluctance, heading to the window while she dashed toward the closet. He waited in breathless silence for the sound of the first firecracker going off.

Even though he was expecting it, the loud bang from the other room made his heart jump. He heard Megan's soft exhalation by the closet. There was a muted click and suddenly, from over their heads came a low, rumbling roar.

More firecrackers exploded, coming from three

different sides of the house. Overhead, there were
thuds as whoever was in the attic reacted to the
whirling fan blade now chopping only inches from
their heads. Behind him, Megan padded quietly
into place, bending down to pick up her bag and
his.

Outside the window, Evan saw movement. The
two men in the woods were running off, one heading to the back of the house, the other toward the
front.

"Now," he whispered to Megan, pulling the
window open. It moved soundlessly, to his relief.

He pushed the screen out. He couldn't hear it hit
the ground over the sound of the firecrackers. He
turned to Megan and lifted her over the sill, bag
and all, then handed her his bag. He climbed out
the window and pulled it closed behind him.

"Go!" he whispered, taking his bag. He slung
the canvas strap over his shoulder and raced after
her into the woods.

They had about a fifty-yard head start and the
advantage of Megan's familiarity with the mountainside. But it didn't take long for their pursuers
to realize they'd been tricked, and about halfway
down the mountain, they heard the sound of bullets
hitting the trees around them, though the sound-
suppressors on the intruders' rifles muted the
shots.

"This way," Megan growled, grabbing his hand.
She took him over a sudden drop of about five feet,

landing like a cat on both feet. He hit more awkwardly, his left ankle twisting.

Luckily for him, they weren't going much farther. She pulled him with her into a small hole in the rocky face of the mountain and flattened her back against the cave wall.

"We should be okay if they don't have dogs," she breathed. "Did you see any dogs?"

"No." He wiggled his ankle, testing it for injury. It was sore but it seemed to function well enough. "We can't hole up here forever."

Her elbow dug into his side as she pulled something from her pocket. Her cell phone—the display panel lit up, bathing her face with blue light. She punched in a number and typed Are you out there?

A few seconds later, her phone buzzed a text reply. East of the cabin. Is that gunfire?

She responded with an affirmative. We're west of the cabin, holed up. Can you draw them off?

The affirmative response was followed quickly by the sound of gunfire to the east. They heard the sound of footsteps crashing through the underbrush outside the cave, closer than expected. Evan's racing pulse ratcheted up another notch.

They waited for what felt like an hour but must have been mere minutes. At some point, Megan got another text message, the hum of her cell phone making them both jump. She read it quickly and didn't comment, just closed the phone and tucked it back in the pocket of her jeans.

With no further noises outside the cave, Evan whispered, "Should we try it now?"

"One at a time, in case there's an ambush."

"I'll go first," he said.

She shook her head. "You're bigger and stronger. You'd have a better chance of rescuing me than vice versa. I'll go first." She gave his hand a hard squeeze, and darted out into the night.

She went forward about ten yards, past his field of vision. His chest tightened with anxiety.

Then she was back. "They seem to be headed east. Let's go while we can."

The run down the mountain was nearly as harrowing as anything he'd experienced during his time in Kaziristan. The pitch-dark night and the lush spring growth in the woods made for treacherous footing.

Megan was as sure-footed as a cat, and apparently as sharp-eyed, as well, for she seemed able to use the faint blue glow of moonlight filtering through the trees to see ahead far better than Evan could. She nimbly sidestepped obstacles that would have sent Evan sprawling face-first into the forest floor. He quickly learned to stay in her wake, letting her search out and neutralize the dangers ahead.

The dangers behind, however, posed a much greater problem. Two-thirds of the way down the mountain, with the lake now visible, gleaming like blue diamonds through the trees, Evan felt something whistle past his head. Nearby, the trunk of a tree shuddered from the impact, spraying splinters outward.

"Go low and zigzag!" he called to Megan, but she was already off like a rabbit, scampering through the underbrush like a wild thing. He and his aching ankle struggled to keep up with her pace, especially since he took a different route to force their pursuers to track two targets instead of one.

He felt another bullet snag the sleeve of his jacket, but he couldn't stop long enough to check if he was hit. He didn't think so—he felt no pain—but adrenaline could be a trickster.

"Here!" He barely heard Megan's whisper over his own thundering pulse. He spotted her ahead and dashed toward her, tripping and sprawling when his foot caught a large tree root sticking out of the soil.

He felt her hands on him, pulling him to his feet, and he gladly took her hand and let her lead the way toward the darkened boathouse he saw just ahead, a simple wood structure on stilts that hung out several feet past the shoreline into the gently lapping water of Lake Gossamer.

"What now?" he asked, crouching behind the large black speedboat moored in the boathouse.

"We get this thing on the water." She was already climbing into the boat, feeling around the interior compartments until she found what she was looking for—a key. "Can you untie the moor rope? We're getting out of here."

He limped over to the post and untied the rope. "Who leaves the key to his boat *in* the boat?"

She flashed him a grin big enough that he could see her white teeth glimmering in the darkness. "My cousin Gabe, when I ask him to." She pocketed the key and went into the well of the boat, coming back with two large oars. "They couldn't have seen where we went after that last turn in the woods, but they'll come looking for us sooner or later. So we take this boat out slow and quiet, okay? Just beyond the point, then I'll engage the trolling motor for a little while after that before trying to start the outboard."

He was glad she knew what she was doing. For all the time he'd spent on lakes and ponds as a kid, he'd never learned much about boats. His family had never been wealthy enough to own one of their own, nor had any of his boyhood friends.

The boat was sleek but large. Rowing their way out of the boathouse without crashing the vessel into the wooden pier took serious effort, the need for quiet forcing them to row longer and more slowly than he'd have liked.

As they neared the point of land jutting out into the lake, he spotted two black-clad men moving stealthily through the woods about a hundred yards from the boathouse, barely visible through the trees. "Get down," he whispered urgently to Megan.

She crouched low in the boat, stopping her rowing, but the forward impetus kept them gliding silently through the water. Evan hoped the boat was as difficult to see as the men were.

The boat slowed, forcing them to risk rowing again. They passed the jutting point of land, putting more distance between themselves and the men skulking through the trees. By now, Evan's muscles burned with exertion, and he could tell from Megan's pinched face that she was beginning to feel the toll of rowing the big bass boat across the murky surface of the lake.

The sound of a couple of fast-moving boats skimming across the water toward them sent Evan's nerves jangling. Soon shouts could be heard, as well, from one boat to the other.

It sounded like some good ol' boys out late fishing, but Evan dropped his hand to his side, where the SIG sat heavy on his hip, looking over his shoulder at the approaching boats.

Megan's hand closed over his on the holster. Turning, he found her crouched beside him, smiling up with gleaming eyes. "It's my cousins Jake and Aaron. They're giving us cover to get out of here." She eased back to the outboard area and put her hand on the trolling motor.

As the boats came nearer, she cranked the trolling motor. It hummed quietly, completely drowned out by the larger outboards of the two bass boats skimming toward them.

The boats slowed as they drew close, giving Megan a chance to put a little distance between herself and the shore without being heard. The two bass boats flanked their boat like an honor guard, throttling their engines down to trolling speed.

All three boats eased their way up the lake until there was no way anyone from the boathouse could possibly see them. Then the bigger of the men—Aaron, Evan remembered—tossed something into their boat and whipped his boat off in another direction.

The other boat settled in beside them, the dark-haired man in the driver's seat nodding at Megan.

She nodded back and put her key in the ignition, starting the outboard engine. The sound was shockingly loud, making Evan wince. She gestured him into the passenger seat and he slid in, giving a wave of gratitude to her cousin Jake.

Jake throttled his engine back up and stayed with them for about a mile as they skated across the water at top speed. Megan handled the large power boat as if she'd been driving them for years—which she probably had, he supposed, remembering how much time she'd spent with her cousins growing up.

She handed him a wad of paper—the thing Aaron Cooper had thrown into the boat, he realized. "Hold this until we're safe to throttle down!" she shouted over the sound of the motor and the wind beating through their clothes and hair.

They neared the dam and she finally pulled back, easing the power boat down until they were moving at a stately pace, barely putting out a wake.

"There's a flashlight in the bin right behind you," Megan told him. "Let's see what that is."

He retrieved the flashlight, and she held it while he unfolded the ball of paper. One page was a map with an X on it. "Map of the lake." He showed her the page.

"That's old Beaver Creek Dam," she said. "All the kids used to go parking up there."

The other two pages were instructions. "It's an email from your brother Jesse. They've spotted guys they're pretty sure are SSU doing surveillance on all of their residences as well as Cooper Security." His throat tightened, feeling the noose. "No coverage on the cousins yet, which is why they sent them to our aid, but he thinks we need to get out of town for a while, until they can figure out what's really going on here."

"Good thing we kept our bags with us," she said.

"He says your cousin Cissy is waiting for us at the dam with her boyfriend, Shane Mason. He's agreed to let us borrow his truck since it's not likely to be easily connected to Cooper Security. We'll take the truck, they'll take the boat back to Cooper Cove Marina." He looked up at Megan, shaking his head. "What are you Coopers, a bunch of secret agents?"

She shot him a wry grin. "Not by choice, believe me."

Beaver Creek Dam was another couple of miles away. They made good time on the first mile and a half, running the boat at full speed. But they had to throttle down again at the mouth of the creek and came to a full stop at a rickety-looking pier that jutted into the wide creek. Standing on the pier, a tall, dark-haired girl of twenty or so and a taller young man with sandy hair wearing a denim jacket were playing a convincing pair of lovers, wrapped around each other in the dark.

They broke apart as the boat idled up to the pier. The girl grinned sheepishly at Megan. "Truck's up at the top of the hill—blue Ford with a flag sticker on the windshield. We parked it away from the other cars up there, but you may want to hold hands or something so nobody looks at you suspiciously. Uncle Luke sent you a pair of cell phones. We left them on the seat. They each have a thousand minutes a month and they're untraceable. He said you should leave your phones with us." She motioned toward the rope coiled at the back of the boat. "Mr. Pike, could you toss me that rope?"

He hurried to get the rope, glad to note his ankle wasn't hurting as much as it had earlier. He threw the girl the rope, and she and her companion pulled the boat flush with the pier.

Megan cut the engine and left the key in the ignition. When she had climbed up to the pier, she gave the girl a hug. "Thank you, Cissy. And you, too, Shane."

The boy smiled at Megan and nodded politely to Evan. "Don't scuff up my truck, okay? It's my baby."

"We'll do the best we can to bring it back in the same condition," Evan promised, remembering how much he'd loved his first truck when he bought it.

After handing over their cell phones as requested, they left the kids with the boat and started up the crooked path. Megan grabbed Evan's hand, as Cissy had suggested. He wasn't sure it was necessary; from what he remembered of his teenage days, the last thing he'd cared about was what other people were doing in their cars on Lovers' Lane.

But he wasn't going to complain about holding Megan's hand.

She snuggled even closer as they reached the top of the rise, where the land flattened to a level dirt parking area on one side of the dam. "I doubt anyone's looking," she murmured, raising her face to him. "But just to be safe—" She rose on her tiptoes and pressed a soft kiss against his lips.

Desire swamped him, flooding his insides with sweet heat. He cupped the back of her head in his palm and held her still, kissing her back with fierce hunger. Only the sound of a car moving along the road nearby drove them apart, and they hurried to the truck, stashing their bags on the bench seat of the extended cab.

"Let's wait here a little while. Don't want to draw too much attention by heading right off," Evan suggested, though he was disappointed to see that, unlike his first truck, this was a newer model with the gear console on the floor between them.

Megan didn't let the console bother her, crawling across the console until she was in his lap. "Put the seat back, she ordered. "The steering wheel's diggin' into my ribs."

He did as she asked, feeling sixteen again, breathless and out of control. Her hot breath mingled with his as she bent and brushed her mouth against his again.

"For show," she whispered, cradling his face in her hands and lowering her mouth to his in a third kiss.

He threaded his fingers through her hair, holding her close, driven by adrenaline and relief and a richer, darker emotion he didn't want to name. She was a live wire beneath his hands, shooting sparks through his system until he thought he would ignite from the inside out.

He was fast losing his hold on the world around him, drowning in her, and that scared the hell out of him.

"No," he gasped, pulling away. "This is not the time to forget ourselves."

Her low groan of frustration rumbled through him. She pressed her forehead to his. "I'm sorry."

He covered her hands where they lay against his cheeks. "Why don't we just get out of here?"

She dropped back into the passenger seat of the truck, her head falling back against the headrest. "Any thoughts where we should go now?"

There was only one place he could think of, one place where even people who knew him well would never think to look for him.

One place he hadn't been since he was seventeen years old and still nothing more than a naive kid from coal country.

He turned and looked at Megan, at her weary expression and the trust that shined like a challenge in her scared gray eyes.

"Yeah. I have an idea." He buckled himself in and cranked the truck. The engine roared to life, its full throttle purr humming in his ears like a hillbilly anthem.

After eighteen years in the wilderness, Evan Earl Pike was going home to Kentucky.

Chapter Twelve

Somewhere around Lenoir City, Tennessee, Megan fell asleep, her head slumped against the truck window, and dreamed.

She was home, at the cozy bungalow in Gossamer Ridge, sitting on the top step of the porch. Vince sat beside her, helping her shell peas into a large white bowl sitting on the step between them. Under his breath, he hummed an old Alabama song—"Dixieland Delight," one of his favorites. He couldn't carry a tune worth a damn, but his enthusiasm was infectious, and she found herself humming along.

"You've been wearin' black long enough, baby." His familiar voice wrapped around her like a cloud.

No, she thought sadly. Like a shroud.

"You've been sleepin' on my grave again." Vince sounded so sad it made her want to cry. "That ain't necessary, you know. I ain't there anymore. You're just lyin' with bones."

Looking down at herself, she saw she was dressed in the black silk dress she'd worn to his funeral, the glossy fabric streaked with the red clay dirt of his grave.

She woke to the sound of rain pattering on the window beneath her head and the soft swish of windshield wipers beating a cadence in rhythm with her heart.

Through the windshield, the headlights illuminated a curvy two-lane highway, flanked on either side with thick woods. Ahead, rain clouds kissed the top of a gentle mountain slope.

She stretched and yawned. "Where are we?"

"Harlan County, Kentucky," Evan answered flatly. He sounded as if he'd just answered, "Hell," instead.

"You never told me why you chose Kentucky," she commented carefully, recognizing quicksand when she saw it.

"Because nobody who knew me would ever think to find me here." His tone discouraged further questions.

By the time they reached the outskirts of Cumberland, Kentucky, the rain had stopped and a watery sunrise struggled to burn through the thinning clouds. Instead of continuing on the highway, Evan pulled the truck down a narrow road into a hollow. She could tell by the tense set of his jaw that he was taking her somewhere familiar to him.

"You're a Kentucky boy," she said softly.

He glanced her way. "You reckon so?" She hardly

recognized his voice, tinted now with a drawl as deep and hard as the hills around them.

"Kentucky's a beautiful state," she ventured.

"Beautiful. And terrible."

"The drug cartel that killed your brother wasn't from South America," she guessed. "Dixie Mafia?"

He shot her a bleak look.

"I'm sorry. My sister Isabel had some trouble with the Alabama version last month."

"Nate wasn't working for a charity. He got sucked into a mess. Mama warned him to stay away from the Bufords. Nate thought he knew what he was doing." Evan shook his head. "We never got to bury him. They threw him in an old mine shaft and collapsed it on top of him. Didn't tell us until it was too late for hope."

"My God."

"Would've put too many people in danger to try to dig his body out, so we left him where he lay."

She reached across the space between them, brushing her fingers down his arm. His jaw tightened, and she dropped her hand away. "How long since you've been here?"

"Eighteen years."

She couldn't imagine being away from Alabama that long. "Do you still have family here?"

"My father moved north years ago," he answered. "My mother lived here until she died a couple of years ago. All that's left here are cousins on her side."

"Any that will help us?"

"Not sure," he admitted. "Daddy never liked Mama's side of the family. I guess he thought he was better than they were—he worked for the mining company. He was from Pittsburgh originally, and I guess deep down he thought he was marrying beneath him when he took a Cumberland girl for his wife."

She grimaced. "Sounds like your mama was the one marryin' down, to me."

He smiled at her. "You might be right."

He reached down and turned on the radio, a burst of static making him grimace. He fiddled with the dial until he found a station playing country music. "When in Cumberland…"

"Where does this road take us?" she asked.

"You'll see."

The road twisted along the flow of a river, taking them deeper into the mountains. It didn't look very different from the hills and hollows of her home in Chickasaw County, but she imagined a stranger like Evan's father might look at the wilderness ahead and think he'd entered another world.

The first sign of civilization in miles loomed in the gray dawn, a small, shabby-looking one-story motel. The marquee outside the small brick building was barely legible, the paint flaked and faded. "Meade Motor Inn," Megan read aloud.

"Everybody calls it MeMo," Evan said. "I wasn't sure it would still be here—it was already on its last legs back when I was a kid. I worked here every summer for three years."

"You weren't sure it would still be here but this is where you thought to run?" She spotted a few cars parked in front of some of the closer rooms, so she supposed the motel still took in guests. Though she had to wonder what sort of travelers a place like this might attract.

Desperate people on the run like her and Evan?

He parked in front of a square building on the near side of the motel. A faded sign reading "Office" hung askew on the blue door. "Stay here," he told her. "I'll be back in a minute."

Megan glanced at her watch as she waited. Almost 6:00 a.m. She wondered doubtfully if a place like the Meade Motor Inn even had a night staff. But Evan came back out in a few minutes, carrying a couple of old-fashioned room keys. "Adjoining rooms," he said, handing her one of the keys. "I figured we'd want to stay close."

His Kentucky drawl was out in full force now, as if he'd decided to drop the pretense. He even looked a little different, she realized as he wheeled the truck around and drove them down to a room at the far end of the motel.

The room Evan unlocked for her was a little on the shabby side but scrupulously clean, the linens on the double bed freshly laundered and smelling like sunshine and mountain air. The carpet under her feet was worn but spotless, and the small bathroom almost sparkled.

"This is nice." She smiled at Evan.

"You sound relieved."

"I am, a little," she admitted. "Is the place under the same management as when you worked here?"

"Yeah, more or less." He picked up his bag and started toward the adjoining doors next to the bathroom.

She caught his arm, stopping him. "Can you stay in here?"

"We could both use a little shut-eye—"

"I know, but could you stay?"

His brow furrowed as he tried to read the meaning behind her request. "Sleep in here with you?"

She knew she was being weak and childish, but she didn't want to be alone right now. She could remember only snippets of her dream about Vince, just enough to leave her feeling scared and unsettled. She had a sick feeling that if she let Evan out of her sight right now, he'd disappear somewhere into the dark hills outside, swallowed whole as his brother had been, and she'd never see him again.

He seemed to read her fear in her eyes, his expression softening. He dropped his bag next to hers by the bed and crossed to the adjoining door to lock it. Returning to her side, he sat on the bed, glancing up as she sat beside him, watching him with sudden wariness.

"I'm just talking about sleep," she said, even though she wasn't sure that was the entire truth.

"I know." He bent and pulled off his dusty boots. "I don't think I'm capable of anything else at the moment."

She pulled off her own tennis shoes and socks. She considered shrugging off her jeans, as well, but decided against it. She stretched out on top of the covers, giving in to the weary ache that seemed to weld her body to the soft mattress.

She found the strength to move, however, when Evan stretched out beside her. The touch of his body to hers blanketed her with welcome heat. She rolled onto her side, nestling her back against his chest. "Is this okay?"

He wrapped his arm around her waist, tucking her closer. "It's just fine," he murmured, his drawl low and sexy in her ear. And if she hadn't just spent the last thirty hours running for her life, she might have found the strength to do something about the slow burn his voice had sparked low in her belly. But weariness won out, and she drifted off into a long, dreamless sleep.

THE SUN WAS ALREADY low in the western sky when Evan awoke, feeling sore but rested. His ankle complained mildly when he stretched it, but he didn't think it would cause him any long-term problems. The empty bed beside him—and the woman who should have been there—posed a much bigger dilemma.

He'd promised himself, after eighteen years of life with two people entirely unsuited to be married to each other, that he was never going to take a chance on such a disaster. Relationships were generally short-lived, in his experience; only a rare few found long-term happiness, and it was a gamble he had no desire to take. He didn't have the energy for relationships with more than one woman at a time, but he made it clear, going in, that he wasn't in it for the long haul. He'd found, with little regret, that relationships based on such shallow foundations usually died quickly enough from starvation.

He never lied about who he was or what he wanted. He'd never once left a woman behind with any regret.

But the mere act of waking up to an empty room, in an empty bed that had once held Megan Randall's sleeping body tucked up close to his own, gnawed a hole of anxiety right through the center of his gut.

He got out of bed and checked the door to the adjoining room. It was unlocked, and the door on the other side was open. From inside the room, he heard the sound of the shower running.

Immediately, he pictured her naked under the spray, her body slick with water. He imagined himself in the shower with her, touching the curve of her hip, the sweet swell of her small, firm breasts.

He forced his mind away from temptation, looking around the room to see if she'd already moved in. Her bag lay open on the bed, but most of her clothes remained inside. And on top of everything sat the rolled-up wad of pages her husband had sent her wrapped up in the belly of a dog toy.

Glad for the distraction, he picked up the pages and carried them over to the small table near the window. He pulled up a chair and spread the pages out, taking a good long look at Vince Randall's small, neat writing.

Megan had already been through the notes thoroughly, and the only thing she'd gleaned of interest was that Evan had seen a State Department official—almost certainly Barton Reid—speaking urgently to a man Vince knew to be a terrorist.

But when he reached that section of the notes, he spotted a name that made him sit up straight.

"Preacher was with me. Saw SDBR with aA. He said not to go to the C.O. with info. Bucking for trouble." Evan read the words aloud, surprised.

"Surprised me, too." Megan's voice made him jump.

He turned to find her wrapped up in a fluffy white towel, her wet hair falling in curls over her bare shoulders. He almost lost his train of thought.

"Surprised you?" he echoed.

"That a chaplain would tell him not to go to his C.O. with that kind of information."

He shook his head, forcing his gaze away from

her long, toned legs. "Preacher wasn't the chaplain. He was your husband's unit captain."

"Captain Gantry?" she asked, confused for a second until the name kicked in. "Oh. *Elmer Gantry.* The preacher."

"Picked up the nickname in college," Evan said. "When your name is Elmore Gantry, there's not much chance you'll get away without some sort of moniker like that."

"So his own captain told him to keep quiet?" She frowned.

"I'd like to know that myself." As far as he knew, Captain Gantry was still in the army. It shouldn't be hard to figure out where he was stationed now. If they were lucky, he'd be stateside somewhere instead of halfway across the world.

Megan picked up the borrowed cell phone from the bed. "Uh-oh," she said, looking at the display. "I missed about a dozen worried phone calls from my family. I'd better call them back before they freak out and call in the FBI." Megan made a face, but he could tell she was also feeling homesick for her overprotective family.

This was his chance to retreat before the continued temptation of her clean, damp body destroyed his better intentions. He headed for the door. "I'll go shower and let you make your calls in peace."

As soon as the door closed behind him, he slipped out of his dirty clothes and stepped into the shower, turning the cold tap up to full.

All the good work the cold shower did in cooling down his slow burn hunger for Megan nearly derailed ten minutes later when she walked into his room without knocking and caught him shirtless. The smolder in her gray eyes almost destroyed his resolve, but he'd made a plan while in the shower that ought to help them get through the rest of the evening unscathed.

"Jesse's going to call back when he gets anything on Gantry," she told him, not bothering to pretend she wasn't ogling him. Her gaze went down to his bare feet and back up again, and a smile touched her mouth. "You work out?"

He made a joke of the question. "Not what you expected from a former Pentagon lawyer?" He pulled on a dark blue polo shirt, well aware it would make him the most overdressed person at the place he was taking Megan for dinner.

When he told her they were going out, she looked surprised. "We're on the run and you're talking about going out to dinner?"

"Dancing, too," he added, enjoying her look of confusion.

"You're going to order pizza and play tunes on your laptop?" she guessed, eyeing his smile with suspicion.

"No, ma'am. We're goin' out." There it was again. The accent he'd spent most of his adult life trying to lose. You could take a boy out of the hills of eastern Kentucky, but you couldn't take those bloody hills out of the boy.

He found it didn't bother him so much, hearing it come out of him so naturally, as if he'd never walked out of these hills and hollows in the first place.

Megan looked down doubtfully at her jeans and blue plaid blouse. "Do I need to change clothes?"

He shook his head. "You look perfect."

Her broad smile was an unexpected reward. But it faded quickly. "We should pack everything back up and take it with us in the truck, in case we have to make a run for it—"

"We're not taking the truck," he said, holding out his hand to her. "Coming?"

She eyed him with suspicion but took his hand and let him lead her outside the motel room.

They didn't go far, just walked the thirty yards from the end of the motel to the office building. By the time they made it halfway, he heard the sound of music coming from inside the office—banjo, fiddle, mandolins and the steely wail of a dobro.

An answering chord vibrated in the center of his chest.

"Bluegrass," Megan murmured, turning shining eyes toward him. "I love bluegrass."

He'd had a feeling she would. A maelstrom of memories—emotions—roiled through him as he opened the blue door and followed her inside.

Chapter Thirteen

Music hit them like a wall of sound, and Megan found her heart quickening to match the driving beat of the banjo picker's flying fingers.

The live band on a circular stage in the middle of the small room consisted of a female fiddler who didn't look a day over thirteen, an older woman on the mandolin, a gangly young man in his early twenties on the bass, and two older men playing dobro and guitar. The banjo picker was another girl, a few years older than the fiddler. Her small, talented fingers were plucking the fire out of her banjo as she ripped through a hyper speed version of "Flint Hill Special."

"I first heard the Meades play when I wasn't much older than the girl on the banjo," Evan said into Megan's ear.

"You know the band?"

"The Meades own MeMo. Have for a couple of generations. The whole family pitches in on upkeep, and they play music in the evenings to help supplement the costs."

A rawboned man in jeans and a plaid shirt approached them, carrying a straw hat. "Ten dollars cover," he said in a mountain drawl that Evan reacted to with a faint smile. Megan wondered what he was thinking.

Evan opened his wallet and withdrew a twenty for the hat, then followed Megan deeper into the crowd milling around the stage, where the band was finishing up the song.

The older woman on the mandolin caught sight of Evan, a broad smile spreading across her lean face. When the last chord died, she said something to the guitar player, who announced they were taking a break.

"Evan Pike! Good lord, boy, I thought you was never comin' back to see us again!" The mandolin player was a tall, lean woman in her late thirties, with honey-brown hair touched with strands of gray and an unvarnished face that was pretty in a vulpine, almost feral way, her beauty more wild than cultured.

Her accent was pure Kentucky, hard-edged and raw. "Del said he seen you early this morning, but when you didn't show up later to say hi, I was afraid you'd done run off again without even sayin' goodbye!" She held him away from her at arm's length, her mandolin tucked up to her side under her arm. "What on earth have you been doin' with yourself all this time?"

"It's a long story, Nola." Evan's accent broad-ened, apparently feeding off Nola's hill country twang. "I was going to say it's great to see nothing much has changed around here, but you have babies now nearly as old as you were the last time I saw you."

"Yeah, they grow up too fast sometimes. Tammie Jane's got her a new boyfriend—it's lookin' real serious now. I'm just hopin' she'll finish up her college before she settles down and starts makin' babies—just started in nursing at the community college. I'm hopin' she'll be able to transfer up to UK next year, if she doesn't get all weddin' crazy." Nola shook her head. "And Dorrie's just made the honors class this year. She's the one on the fiddle." She looked past him to Megan, her warm brown eyes looking her over thoroughly. "Good lord, listen to me babblin' on and on in front of your friend!"

Evan met Megan's questioning gaze. "Nola, this is Megan Randall. Megan, this is Nola Dalton Meade and her brood. Her husband Del's family has run this place for years." Evan looked back at Nola. "Megan's husband was…a friend of mine."

Nola quickly picked up on the past tense. "I see."

"Vince was in the army." Megan left it at that.

"I'm helping her work through some leftover issues from his combat death," Evan added. Not the whole truth, but close enough, Megan thought. "It's a sensitive matter, so we're trying to keep our presence here low-key."

Nola's eyebrows rose. "Well, you came to the wrong place for low-key, sugar." She waved around at the noisy room.

The Meade Motor Inn had apparently turned their check-in office into a bluegrass music hall. There was a bar to one side, though Megan didn't see any alcohol being served. Harlan County must be dry, like Chickasaw County was. But if anyone in the place felt in need of spirits, they seemed to be getting all they wanted from the bluegrass music the Meades had been playing, as authentic as she'd ever heard.

She saw Evan's gaze wander down to the mandolin in Nola's hands. He gave a small start of surprise. "Is that a Chesterfield?"

Nola's dark eyes met his, crinkling with a smile. "It is, indeed."

Megan looked closer at the mandolin and saw the Chesterfield mark. "But it looks brand-new."

Nola and Evan both looked at Megan with surprise. "You know about Chesterfields?" Nola asked.

Megan nodded. "I worked at a bluegrass music hall in Nashville when I was in college. Had a friend who swore by Chesterfield mandolins— said she wouldn't buy any other kind."

"I bought it from Evan's cousin Cecil last year." Nola turned her gaze to Evan. "Cecil's picked up where your Uncle Thomas left off. Doin' a real fine job." Her expression fell. "We was real sorry to hear about your uncle's passing. The Chester-fields are like bluegrass royalty around here."

"You're a Chesterfield?" Megan asked Evan.

He nodded. "On my mama's side."

"His uncle Thomas made some of the finest mandolins you can find anywhere, but you practically had to beg him to do it, no matter how much you offered to pay." Nola laughed. "They do say the real geniuses are usually odd birds. Your cousin Cecil's turning out to be the same way, Evan."

"May I see it?" Evan asked, an odd light in his eyes, as if his fingers were itching to run across the double strings.

"Sure." Nola handed the instrument over.

Megan watched with interest as he settled his fingertips over the steel strings. He was rusty—she wondered if he'd played in years—but it didn't take long for him to coax a few measures of "Blue Moon of Kentucky" out of the instrument.

"Should have known a Chesterfield would still know his way around a mandolin," Nola said, clapping with delight. "Do you play, Mrs. Randall?"

"Please, call me Megan," she said quickly, her smile warm. She liked Nola Meade, she decided. "And no, I don't play mandolin. I can pick a little guitar, and I used to sing—"

"Then you'll have to sing for us tonight!" Nola exclaimed, clapping her hands.

Megan looked up at Evan, alarmed. "Oh, no, I haven't sung in forever—"

"You sing?" Evan asked, his fingers still darting over the strings, making up a tune as they went.

"Not anymore."

"You could sing with her," Nola suggested. She put her hand on Megan's arm, her voice dipping conspiratorially. "Back when Evan was working for Del's daddy, the Meades used to have an open mic night on Thursdays and he'd come sing every time. You want to give it a go again, Evan?"

"It's not Thursday," he said with an indulgent smile. "But we sure would like to dance to some of your music." He slipped his hand into Megan's. "Something nice and slow would be good."

Nola smiled at him. "You ain't changed a bit, Evan Earl Pike." But she climbed back up on the stage, murmured something to the man holding the enormous bass fiddle and the Meades started playing a sultry rendition of "The Tennessee Waltz."

"I'm a terrible dancer," Megan warned Evan as he pulled her into his arms. But she couldn't help smiling as the music lightened her mood better than any happy pill could.

Evan was a good dancer, moving with a light, easy rhythm that made her feel as if she were moving on air. He pulled her against him more tightly, nuzzling her hair.

"Why did you leave Kentucky?" she murmured against his throat. "Because of your brother's death?"

She felt his steps falter for a second before he

recovered. "Nate was supposed to be the one who made it. He was going to college, on his way to a real life that didn't include coal mines or farming. But he never could turn his back on a friend. One of his high school buddies roped him into a plan to steal a big shipment of pot the Bufords were sending across state. It was going to be a big score—enough money to pay his tuition for an extra year. Nate thought he could do this one thing, make all that money and it would be done—"

"Never works out that way." Growing up in rural Alabama, Megan had seen her share of big dreams colliding with reality.

Evan's body was tense with anger. "Nate threw away a life that would have been worth living. Drove the final nail in the coffin of my parents' marriage."

"I'm sorry."

"I got out of here as soon as I could. I wanted it behind me. And then I went out and got the education he should have gotten, the law degree he wanted—" He shook his head.

"Is it what *you* wanted?" Megan leaned her head back to look into his eyes. "Being a lawyer?"

He frowned. "I thought it was at the time. But I've been thinking of a change."

"No more lawyering?"

"Certainly not the kind of lawyering that makes you tell a soldier to hold his fire when people are shooting at him," he said darkly. He forced a smile. "Am I too old to join the FBI this late in life?"

"I'm not sure you'd enjoy their rules any more than the Pentagon's," Megan warned. "At least, that's what my sister Izzy says."

"Does she ever regret leaving the FBI?"

Megan shook her head, thinking how happy her sister was now that she and Ben Scanlon were back together again. "She's working with her partner again, now that Ben's joined us at Cooper Security, so she still has everything she loved most about working at the FBI."

The slow song came to an end, and on stage, Nola shot them an apologetic look as the band went immediately into a lightning-paced "Fox on the Run."

"You hungry?" Evan asked, waving toward the bar. Besides offering soft drinks, juice, tea and coffee, the Meade Motor Inn apparently served food, if the chalkboard menu over the bar was anything to go by.

"Starving," she answered, realizing they hadn't eaten since the quick burger they'd grabbed on the drive home from Nashville the day before.

The menu wasn't extensive or fancy, but Megan was delighted to find a fried bologna sandwich on the menu. "It was Dad's go-to dinner when we were kids," she admitted with a grin. She ordered the sandwich and a glass of iced apple cider, while Evan opted for the fried catfish sandwich and root beer. They found a small table near the back of the room and ate their first meal in over twenty-four hours.

Full and feeling relaxed for the first time in days, Megan pulled Evan out on the dance floor again for the next song, "Dumas Walker," and coaxed him into a pretty creditable two-step. By the time the song ended, he was laughing almost as hard as she was.

"My ankle is going to hate me in the morning," he groaned as he limped back to their table. "But that was fun."

Megan realized she hadn't laughed so much, or felt so lighthearted, in years.

Four years, to be exact. Since Vince's death.

"It was," she agreed, her smile faltering only a little.

He reached across the table and took her hand. "I know it's just an oasis, but I think I needed a night like this."

Just an oasis. The full weight of the secret forces aligned against them settled on her shoulders, dimming her contentment. "I did, too, but we should head back to the room now. And maybe remind Nola not to tell anybody you're back in Kentucky?"

"They'll keep it quiet," he assured her. "Not the first time someone in these parts needed to stay under the radar." He stood, holding out his hand. "Let's go say good-night."

She slipped her hand into his and they crossed to

the stage, where the Meades were winding down another song. Nola and her husband both stepped down from the stage to say good night.

"You reckon you'll be stickin' around past to-night?" Nola asked hopefully.

"Not sure how long we'll be here," Evan answered, apology in his voice. He gave her a hug. "Good to see both of you again. I'll try not to be such a stranger in the future."

"I'm gonna hold you to that, Evan." Nola's husband, Del, shook Evan's hand firmly. He was a beanstalk of a man with a plain face made distinctive by soulful brown eyes. He turned those eyes on Megan as he bid her farewell, and she could see how he'd caught Nola's attention in the first place.

"I like your friends," she told Evan as they walked hand in hand down the motel breezeway. "And I can't believe you're a mandolin player."

"I haven't played in years," he said, smiling slightly. "When I left Kentucky, I left it all."

Something about the tone of his voice made her think he was beginning to regret that decision. "You could ask your cousin to make you a new one."

He shot her a wry smile as she unlocked the door to her room. "I'm unemployed at the moment. I don't think I could afford Cecil's prices."

"There's a good secondhand shop back in May-bridge, not far from the office," she said as they went inside. "I've seen pretty decent-looking mandolins for sale there before—"

He caught her face between his hands and smiled down at her. "You don't have to fix me all at once, Megan."

"Sorry." She chuckled ruefully. "I tend to tackle problems when I see them."

His thumbs moved lightly across her cheeks. "And you see a problem in me?"

"Is that an honest question?" she asked.

He cocked his head. "I guess it is."

"I think you had a sad childhood in a lot of ways, and you blame it all on this place, so when you got the chance, you wiped the dirt of Kentucky off your feet and got the hell out. You pretended you were from somewhere else, cut yourself off from everyone and everything that reminded you of home—"

He dropped his hands away from her face, turning away. Regret bridled her tongue—she had a bad habit of being a little too honest when discretion might stand her in better stead.

"The accent was the hardest to get rid of." He unlocked the motel room door. "You see how easily I slip back into it. I thought I'd finally conquered it by the time I started working at the Pentagon, but half of everyone I met in the military seemed to be from somewhere south of the Mason-Dixon line." Laughing ruefully, he dropped onto the end of the bed. "By the time I left Kaziristan, I sounded like a Cumberland boy again."

She sat next to him. "You sound a lot like a Cumberland boy now, you know."

He leaned toward her, his shoulder nudging hers. "That's your fault, Dixie. And I guess living in North Carolina for the last year hasn't helped."

She smiled. "I like your accent. It gives you character."

He looked at her with a wry smile. "I like yours, too. It's real and honest." His eyes darkened to a smoky olive. "And incredibly sexy."

The room heated up in a heartbeat. "Evan—"

He threaded his fingers through her hair, drawing her closer. His drawl lowered to a feral growl that sent a tremble of desire rocketing straight to her core. "I know this is all kinds of wrong, but no matter how many times I tell myself so, it doesn't change a thing. I still want you."

She closed her eyes, struggling with her body's reckless response to his touch. "I haven't—not since—"

"I know. I know it should matter—" His words faltered as his lips touched hers. Lightly, a brush. An accidental collision.

But the second touch was deliberate. Commanding. He claimed her mouth with ruthless intent, branding her, demanding surrender. She had no fight left, no desire to resist his conquest. The passion his touch awakened felt as desperate as if she'd taken her first breath after years of drowning.

She slipped her hand under his shirt, her fingers exploring the hard contours of his stomach, the broad expanse of his chest. He groaned, the sound rumbling through her, and she felt the full power of her femininity in his trembling response.

He regained control, laying her back on the bed, pinned beneath his weight. She drank in the desire in his eyes, remembering with a thrill what it was like to be the object of such fiery passion.

His hand shook as he unbuttoned the first button of her shirt. She could see the struggle in his expression, the need for control battling with the need for release. As his fingertip brushed across the swell of her breast, she wasn't sure which side she wanted to win the war.

She felt a brief vibration where his hips pressed into hers. Then another, more powerful.

Evan froze above her, gazing down at her with a puzzled look. Then he started to laugh, rolling aside.

The vibration repeated. This time she also heard the insistent buzz.

Her cell phone was ringing on vibrate.

"Better get that," Evan said, breathless and still chuckling.

Growling with frustration, she dug the phone from her pocket. "Yeah?"

"Did you have to run for the phone?" Jesse asked. "You sound out of breath."

Heat poured into her cheeks and down her neck. "Somethin' like that. Do you have news?"

"Well, yeah, as a matter of fact. Is Pike where he can hear if you put me on speaker?" Jesse asked.

Megan slanted her eyes toward Evan, who still lay on his back next to her on the bed, a rueful smile on his flushed face. "Yeah, he can hear you." She engaged the speaker. "Go ahead."

"We tracked down Captain Gantry." Jesse's voice sounded a little tinny through the cell phone's speaker. "Or, I guess I should say, Major Gantry. He got promoted and transferred out of Kaziristan not long after Vince's death to work at PKSOI in Carlisle, Pennsylvania."

"PKSOI?" Megan asked.

"The army's Peacekeeping and Stability Operations Institute," Evan contributed. "Is he still in Pennsylvania? If we leave first thing in the morning, we could be there before nightfall—"

"Actually, Gantry left PKSOI last year for a new position at Fort Bragg in North Carolina," Jesse said. "Which means—"

"If we leave at dawn, we can meet with Gantry sometime around lunchtime tomorrow," Evan finished for him, his eyes glittering with excitement.

Megan tried to feel the same anticipation, but the closer she got to the answers about Vince's death, the more she wondered if she'd be happy when she found them. Did she really want to know that people high in her own government had ordered her husband's murder?

And did she really want to say goodbye to Evan Pike?

Chapter Fourteen

Evan sat up on the edge of the bed and jotted the contact information Jesse Cooper gave them over the phone, his mind racing ahead to how he wanted to approach Elmore Gantry. The captain—major now—had always been hard to read for Evan. He hadn't been hostile, the way many of the men in his unit had been, but Gantry had never seemed open or friendly, either.

He hadn't been a hard-core disciplinarian by any stretch—he'd trusted his soldiers to do their jobs well and intervened only if there was a mistake or infraction. Nor had he been one of those officers who tried to treat his men like friends. He'd socialized with officers only, but on even those occasions his participation had seemed more a matter of obligation on his part than pleasure.

He'd seemed perpetually preoccupied. Guarded, even. Which might suggest he'd been forced to keep secrets from his men.

Secrets about the upper brass's decision to negotiate with the al Adar rebels?

It wouldn't be easy to get him to speak to them on a good day. And Evan had a feeling the last thing Gantry wanted to discuss was Vince Randall's death. It had been the only live-fire death his unit had suffered under his watch, despite the dangers inherent in peacekeeping duties in Kaziristan.

"You probably shouldn't give Gantry any time to make himself scarce," Jesse warned.

"True," Evan said, though he wasn't really sure Jesse Cooper was right. Trying to beard the lion in his den wasn't usually the best angle of attack. He might do better if he lured Gantry out of his comfort zone.

"Are you still seeing signs of being followed?" Megan asked her brother.

"They're definitely out there. Right now we haven't decided how we want to handle things—clearly, they're not trying to make any moves on any of us. They're just watching."

"We're the ones they want," Megan said. She hadn't bothered to close her shirt, and the tempting sight of her breasts, barely encased by white silk and lace, was beginning to become too potent a distraction for Evan.

He got up from the bed and crossed to the chair by the window, needing the distance. "That suggests we're definitely on the right track with this, doesn't it?"

"I hope so. The more I learn about Barton Reid, the more convinced I become that he should be behind bars for life," Jesse answered flatly. "So far, the SSU isn't watching the Gossamer Lake Coopers. We put them on alert, but they've been combing the woods looking for any sign of intruders and haven't seen a thing. Nobody's going to get past a Cooper on Gossamer Mountain for long, so it seems the SSU is focusing on the immediate family only for now."

Megan looked across at Evan. He dragged his gaze guiltily from her chest to her face, and she blushed, pulling her blouse together. "We should take advantage of that," she suggested.

"Already on it. Luke will be calling you as soon as we get off the phone," Jesse said. "Listen, these people are serious. Don't take any crazy chances. I get why you don't want to bring the authorities in on this right now—I do. But none of this is going to bring Vince back, and I'd just as soon not lose you, too, Red. You hearin' me?"

Megan's eyes glittered brightly with unshed tears, but she squared her jaw and didn't let them spill. "I hear you."

Jesse's voice softened. "Isabel said to tell you Patton's doing fine but he misses you like crazy."

"That's such a lie—Patton thinks Isabel hung the moon," Megan replied with a watery laugh. "Tell her to pet him extra for me. And y'all be safe, too. Just because those goons aren't making a move on any of you now doesn't mean they won't change tactics if they get desperate."

"Believe me, none of us are taking anything for granted." Jesse's tone was utterly grim. "Take care of yourselves, okay? I'll get off the phone now so Luke can get through to you."

"Thanks, Jesse. I love you."

"Love you, too, Red." Jesse hung up, and Megan closed her phone, cradling it to her chest.

Evan watched her struggle for control, acutely aware of how hard it had been to hang up the phone and sever the connection between her and her family. Despite her obvious strength—both physical and mental—their hurried flight from Alabama was starting to take a heavy toll on her.

Just three days ago, she was a widow visiting her husband's grave, with no thought about murders or conspiracies. He'd asked a lot of her when he challenged her to give him ten minutes of her time to listen to his crazy theory.

He'd asked enough.

The phone rang again. Megan grabbed it on the first ring and left it on speakerphone. "Hello?"

"Hi, Megan, it's Luke."

Evan searched his memory, trying to place which cousin was Luke. The guy with the riding barn? He thought that was right.

"J.D., Gabe and Jake are here with me," Luke added. "We're going to try to help you out. Jesse says you're planning to go to Fort Bragg?"

"Right, but we're a lot closer than y'all are." She looked up at Evan. "We're not sure it's a good idea to wait here much longer. Evan's from here, and while he hasn't lived here for a long time, they might still think to look for us here."

"I've got a bird at my disposal." That was a different voice, a low drawl that Evan couldn't place.

"J.D., I can't ask you—" Megan protested.

J.D. was the oldest of the Cooper Cove bunch. The former navy helicopter pilot.

"You aren't asking. I'm offering," J.D. said firmly. "Your brother's already paid for the fuel and my time is my own. Billy's letting me use the LongRanger—six passenger. Practically a luxury model."

The tears Megan had been fighting crept down her cheeks. "Thank you. Is there a particular place you want to meet us?"

"Let me look at the map a minute." On the Alabama end of the call came the rattle of a computer keyboard. "Okay, looks like Wytheville, Virginia, would be on your driving route. I have an old navy buddy who has a transport service and landing strip up there. I can get him to clear me a place on the strip to put down and y'all can meet us there."

Evan's mind raced ahead, realizing Megan's cousins were, unwittingly, giving him exactly the chance he needed to get Megan safely out of the mess he'd brought into her life. "That sounds perfect," he said aloud. "Thank you."

"I'll work things out with my buddy and text you the details before morning," J.D. said.

"What time do y'all plan to hit the road?" Luke asked.

Megan looked at Evan. "We can be up by five. We're on eastern time here, right?"

Evan nodded. "Four in Alabama."

"We should still beat you there by helicopter," J.D. said. "Look for the text from me."

They said their goodbyes, and Megan pocketed her phone again. "This is happening fast," she said, a little breathless.

Too fast, he thought. He pushed to his feet and headed for the door to the adjoining room. "We'd better get some sleep. Five o'clock will come early."

She intercepted him before he reached the door, catching his hand in hers. She gazed up at him with eyes that shined like molten silver. "If Jesse hadn't called—"

He squeezed her hand. "It's probably a good thing he called," he said softly. "Don't you agree?"

She licked her lips, looking as conflicted as he felt. "Yeah. I do. This is a crazy time and a crazy situation. Not a good time for taking big steps."

He knew he should let go of her hand and walk away, take her assent for what it was. But there was pain in her eyes as well as understanding, a pain that he felt echoing in the cavern of his chest.

He caught her face between his hands, bending to press his forehead to hers. Struggling to find words that would erase that pain, he discovered that such words didn't exist. So he just touched his lips to hers in a sweet, undemanding kiss.

A kiss that felt as final as a heartbreak.

Then he hurried to his room, shutting and locking the door behind him.

He walked unsteadily to the bed and sat, pulling out the borrowed cell phone. The contact number for Elmore Gantry was the first thing that came up when he turned on the phone.

Jesse Cooper had said he should wait, not give Gantry time to run. But Jesse didn't know Elmore Gantry. Evan had spent two years working alongside the man.

There were two possibilities here, as far as Evan saw it. Either Gantry was completely innocent and he'd want to help Evan any way he could—or he was still working with the remnants of MacLear and would meet Evan as part of an ambush. No matter which was true, Gantry would agree to meet with Evan.

Either way, Evan thought, he planned to keep Megan out of the line of fire.

MEGAN HAD ANOTHER DREAM of Vince. She dreamed of him often since his death, peaceful dreams where he came to her, perhaps at the home they'd shared, perhaps in the backyard while she was playing with Patton. Sometimes he walked with her through the woods in front of their house or sat with her on the bank of Missacoula Creek while she fished for bluegills.

This time, she was standing on the wood bridge over Crybaby Falls, tossing leaves into the falls, watching them spill down into the creek below and eddy away in violent circles. He joined her on the bridge, coming near enough to touch her if he wanted. But he didn't touch her this time.

"It's okay to let go." His voice was gentle, much more so than it had ever been in life. It always sounded that way in her dreams, as if he'd found his peace and didn't need to struggle so much anymore.

"I don't want to," she protested.

"You want to. But you're afraid."

"People go their whole lives without finding someone who gets who they really are and loves them for it." She shook her head. "It doesn't happen twice. It just doesn't. And I don't want anything else."

"How do you know we really got each other, baby?" His voice remained gentle, but there was a thread of steel beneath, a reminder of the man of strength and action he'd been in life. "We spent more time apart than together. In a whole lot of ways, we barely knew each other at all. We were always more an idea than a reality. That's what you don't want to let go of, darlin'. The idea of us."

Tears ached behind her eyes. "Don't say that."

"It is true. You know it's true." His voice soft-

ened again, grew lush with the love she knew he
had for her. "I believe we'd have been happy our
whole life together, baby. I do. We loved each other.
We'd have chewed away at whatever problems
came up until we made it work. But you're letting
yourself make our relationship into something it
never was."

"It was magic. *We* were magic."

The smile that split his face made her heart hurt.
"All love is magic in the beginning. You can find
that magic again, you know. You can find something that makes you do things you never thought
you could. All you've gotta do is let go of what you
wanted us to be and realize what we really were."

"What were we?" She wiped her eyes but the
tears kept falling, hot on her cheeks.

"We were a couple of Alabama kids who fell in
love, got married and figured we'd eventually get
the chance at forever, once all the other stuff in our
lives finally got out of the way. We just didn't get
the time."

"We should have!" she cried.

"I know. We should've. But we didn't. And I'm
good where I am. Really, baby, I am. But you've
still got years to go, and you may tell yourself
you're the kind of person who can live those years
happily alone, but you're not happy, are you?"

She looked away from his earnest gaze, un-
nerved by the truth she saw in those familiar brown
eyes. "No."

"You buried yourself with me. But there's not enough room for both of us in that grave."

Megan jerked awake, her throat aching with grief. She had fallen asleep atop the covers of the motel bed, still dressed. Lifting her hands to her face, she felt tears on her cheeks.

The dream lingered, vivid and haunting.

You buried yourself with me.

Maybe it was true. Maybe the reason she made daily visits to his grave was that it was where she felt most at home. Her time in the world—with her family, with her dog, going to her job and taking care of her house—those were the between times. The time in transit.

Between visits to her graveyard home.

She shuddered at the thought, a flicker of memory from an earlier dream dancing through her head.

You're just lyin' with bones.

Her gaze wandered across the room to the adjoining doors. What would Evan do if she walked through that door right now? He'd said all the right things, all the noble things, and she couldn't help but admire him for it.

But if she made the move, if she removed the barriers, would he let her stay the night?

She felt so alone. And maybe that wasn't the best reason to push the attraction between them to a more intense level, but she wasn't sure she cared anymore.

She was tired of sleeping with bones.

She pushed herself up off the bed and walked slowly, deliberately to the adjoining door. Closed her hand over the door knob, twisted it, pulled the door open.

And found another closed door.

She almost laughed at the anticlimax. And while a noisy, desperate voice inside her head told her to consider it a sign, she shoved that voice away and turned the knob of the door on Evan's side.

It was locked.

She waited, knowing he'd surely heard the rattle of the knob. Would he come and open it?

She waited, beyond all good sense. And he didn't come.

Releasing a soft breath, she closed the door on her side and leaned her back against the solid wood, feeling like an idiot. He'd made his intentions clear when he'd walked away—he wasn't in the market for complications. And her loneliness didn't change a thing. It was her problem, not his.

She stripped off the clothes that still smelled like him and crawled under the covers alone.

EVAN PAUSED WITH HIS HAND on the phone, realizing that whatever he chose to do next could have far-reaching ramifications. If he ditched Megan at the Wytheville airstrip, she might never forgive him for the betrayal. Telling her he'd made his choice out of concern for her well-being might not be as compelling an excuse to her as it was to him.

Likewise, if he took her with him, she might be walking straight into an ambush.

He quickly dismissed the latter idea. He'd rather she hate him than to see her gunned down in his pursuit of absolution.

That's what it was, really, wasn't it? When he pushed away the nobler sounding excuses, like justice and payment for crimes, all that was really left, all that undergirded his actions for the past few years, was a wretched sense of guilt for Vince Randall's death.

He'd wanted to believe there was evil at work. He'd wanted Vince's death to be someone else's fault.

Funny—now that he was almost certain he was right, that Vince's death had been anything but a simple combat fatality, guilt burned only that much more fiercely in his belly.

A soft rattle drew his gaze back to the adjoining door. He saw the door knob twist slightly, hampered by the lock.

His heart flew into his throat as he realized Megan must be standing on the other side.

Wanting in.

He closed his eyes. Forced himself to remain where he was, even though his entire body seemed to strain toward the barrier between them.

He'd made his decision.

He listened in silence until he heard the faint whisper of her footsteps walking away from the door. A moment later, he thought he could hear the sound of her bed springs creaking.

He opened his eyes and picked up his phone. Punching in the number Jesse had given him, he waited for Gantry to answer.

A woman's voice greeted him on the third ring. "Hello?"

Evan fought the urge to hang up without speaking. "May I speak to Major Gantry?"

"May I tell him who's calling?" the woman asked, wary.

He debated lying but decided to take a gamble. "Tell him it's Evan Pike. We served together in Kaziristan."

"Oh." He could tell by her tone that she recognized his name. He couldn't say for sure whether her reaction was positive or negative. Apparently not negative enough to slam the phone in his ear. "Hold a moment."

He held on, trying to figure out his best approach. Ease into the subject with a little small talk about days gone by? Or jump right into it?

He didn't get the chance to choose. Major Gantry's slow Texas drawl came over the line a moment later, raw with tension. "Evan Pike. Took you long enough. I reckon I've been expecting this call for the past four years."

Chapter Fifteen

Morning dawned gray with hints of rose in the sky above the mountains east of the Meade Motor Inn. Though the hills here were a little higher than back home in Gossamer Ridge, Megan was used to sunrises taking their own sweet time topping the rise. She was also accustomed to fog, living so near Lake Gossamer, but she didn't protest when Evan insisted on taking the wheel for the first leg of the trip to North Carolina.

They said their goodbyes to Del and Nola Meade, who'd made a point to be there for the early shift to see them off. Evan had called them the night before to let them know they'd be checking out at dawn.

"Promise me y'all won't be strangers!" Nola hugged Evan first, then turned to Megan, embracing her like an old friend. "All either one of you have to do is give us a call and we'll find you a room. Maybe stay longer next time so we can take you hiking up at Kingdom Come State Park."

Megan glanced at Evan and found him looking at the floor. Was he trying to avoid meeting her gaze?

Stop it. Not everything is about you.

Except, she was pretty sure his discomfort this morning had everything to do with her, with what they'd come very close to doing the night before.

Locking his door had been a pretty blatant no.

He had been careful not to touch her this morning, treating her with the same formal politeness that had characterized their first interactions. Almost back to Mr. Pike and Mrs. Randall.

She should be glad—she'd been in a vulnerable place last night, drowning in loneliness and need. Any decision she'd have made in that state was almost guaranteed to be a mistake. Evan had saved her from herself. She ought to feel grateful.

Instead, she wanted to smack him upside the head for stirring up a part of her that she'd thought was long dead, then walking away, leaving her hot and frustrated.

Their drive east took them for miles along twisting mountain roads, through scenery as wild and beautiful as anything Megan had seen back home in Chickasaw County. They crossed into Virginia about twenty-five minutes into the drive.

"I had no idea how gorgeous this part of the country was," she ventured after another half hour of silence.

He glanced at her. "Beauty can be deceiving."

His answer irritated her. "You're determined to see only the ugliness. Was your life back there really that terrible?"

A muscle twitched in his jaw, and on the steering wheel, his fingers tightened until his knuckles went white. "Not everyone grows up in a happy family."

She could see the moment he realized his error. His gaze flashed back to her, looking sheepish.

"I'm sorry. I know your mom left and I don't suppose that was exactly a sunny moment," he murmured.

"No."

"But you had your dad. Your brothers and sisters. You said you had aunts and uncles who filled in the blanks your mother left. I had a reclusive uncle I never saw and cousins I've never even met. My dad had no interest in maintaining a relationship with me after Nate died." He shook his head. "I hear the word *Kentucky* and all I think about is how easily my brother got sucked into the drug culture in the mountains. My dad wanted us to leave, to go somewhere with opportunities, but my mother was born here and was determined to die here."

She felt a flutter of pain in the center of her chest, realizing she understood his mother better than he did. She felt that way about Gossamer Ridge. Home was a part of her. She'd lived away from Chickasaw County from time to time, but home always called her back. It had been something else she and Vince had in common.

"You can't forgive her for it," she murmured.

"I didn't say that."

He didn't have to. His bitterness was written all over his grim face.

She remembered their earlier drive through the eastern hills, a breathtaking vista spread before them—lush spring growth, towering pines, mist-tipped mountains rolling across the horizon like folds of pale blue velvet. "You see no beauty at all? You don't get what called to her? What kept her there?"

"Of course I do!" His voice rose with anger. "But I don't understand why she chose it over me."

Megan couldn't hold back a bleak smile. "My mother did the same thing, really. But instead of choosing a place, she chose adventure and her career over us."

"You don't blame her for that?" he challenged.

"Do I wish she'd been a loving, nurturing mother? Of course." Megan had wished for that very thing so many years it hurt to think about it. "But once I grew up and saw how much damage a bad mother can do, I realized my mother did the only thing she knew to do. She wasn't going to be a good mom to us if she stuck around. She'd feel stifled and angry and resentful, and she'd probably take it out on all of us. Then we'd all be miserable."

"Why did she have children if she didn't want them?"

"She loved my dad, and he wanted lots of kids. So she gave them to him."

"And then split?"

"Did I tell you they're not divorced?"

He shot her a look of surprise.

"They don't want to be with other people. They just can't live together. But she calls him all the time. They'll sometimes talk for hours."

"But she doesn't call the rest of you?"

"I think that's probably more our fault than hers. We were so hurt and confused, none of us wanted to talk to her when she'd call."

"But your dad was okay with it?"

"Not at first." She gazed down the highway, saw the rough-hewn cliffs where the road had been cut through an immovable mountain. Her father had been that immovable mountain. He'd been born in Chickasaw County, and he'd die there. Her mother had been looking for a road out. "I think he realized relationships don't have to come in the same boring sizes. As far as I know, he and my mother have been utterly faithful to each other."

"Really." Skepticism colored his flat response.

"Really." She couldn't tamp down a shudder. "And they still have sex when she visits, as I discovered one day much to my mortification."

That earned her a smile from him. "Ugh."

"Yeah. But it works for them. Maybe not for any

of us kids, but it's the compromise they came up with so that they would never really lose each other as long as they were both alive." She found herself smiling. "It's kind of romantic, in a weird way."

"That's very evolved of you."

"I think it took being married to a soldier to make me understand," she admitted. "Vince and I were married three years. We'd dated off and on for a few years before that—off and on not because we were dating other people but because he was in the army."

"I guess he was away almost as much as he was around?"

"More." A snippet of the dream she'd had the night before flashed through her mind. "It makes me wonder—" She stopped, not sure he really wanted to hear such a personal thought.

"Wonder what?" he asked when she didn't go on.

"I just wonder what kind of relationship Vince and I would have had if he'd always been around."

"You think it might have been different?"

"Well, yeah." Since he'd sounded interested, she ventured a little further. "Maybe it would have been better—everything we already were, multiplied by all the extra days of togetherness. Or maybe…"

"You'd get on each other's nerves?" he supplied.

"We did that already," she said with a smile. "But maybe we'd find out that all we really shared was enough love for moments and days at a time. Not a lifetime."

Evan shook his head. "You'd make it work."

"Guess we'll never know."

To her surprise, after so keeping such deliberate distance all morning, Evan reached across the truck cab and pressed the back of his hand to her cheek. "You're a beautiful woman, Megan. You've got a lot of love to give some lucky man. You just have to be open to it."

"Like you are?" The minute she said the words aloud, she clamped her mouth shut. "Sorry."

He dropped his hand back to the steering wheel. "My life is complicated."

"Ambition overcoming any desire to settle down?" His years at the Pentagon pegged him as a man trying to rise in the world. She imagined having to compete with all that ambition might be a losing battle.

"I guess." He didn't seem inclined to continue the discussion, so she settled back against her seat again, trying not to let the tense silence color her mood.

But it was a great relief, two and a half hours later, to read the sign telling them Wytheville was dead ahead.

EVAN TRIED TO KEEP HIS breathing calm and even as they exited the interstate and headed east toward the private airfield where J.D. Cooper and his brothers were waiting for their arrival. J.D. had texted over a set of detailed instructions that would take them from the interstate to the sprawling farm where his buddy kept his plane.

He was doing the right thing. The only thing.

"There's the sign." When Megan spoke, her voice sounded subdued. He knew his silent treatment was behind her reticence, but he hadn't known what else to do.

When she'd asked about ambition overcoming any need to settle down, the question had hit him like a gut punch. Not because it was any big revelation. He'd known for years that career drive was part of his trouble maintaining relationships.

But for the first time he could remember, he felt a deep sense of dissatisfaction with the way he was living his life.

He'd spent so long focused on his career path that only her questions, her challenges, had forced him to look outside his tunnel vision and realize what he was really doing.

He wasn't building a career. He was living another man's life, the life his brother hadn't survived to experience.

His dreams, his ambitions—they were Nate's dreams. Nate's ambitions. Nate had wanted to be a lawyer. Nate had wanted to move to Washington, D.C. Nate had wanted to work at the Pentagon. Nate had wanted out of the hollows and hills of eastern Kentucky, and even the last act of his life, that last score for a big paycheck, had been all about getting out.

Until Nate's death, Evan had never even thought about living anywhere else. He'd loved the harsh, beautiful wilderness, the slow pace of life. He'd loved sitting on the front porch with his mother, shelling peas and shucking corn and listening to her fanciful tales of mountain life.

He'd learned to play the mandolin at his uncle's knee. Learned to ride horses from Delbert Meade, whose family inn had once owned a stable for visitors, back in the day.

He'd followed another man's dream so long, he'd nearly lost sight of his own. Thanks to Megan Randall, he'd begun to realize just what he'd left behind. What he wanted back.

What he was about to throw away.

"There it is." Megan pointed toward a sleek gray helicopter sitting in the middle of a flat, paved square about fifty yards from a modest ranch-style house. Several men milled around the chopper. Evan thought he could make out J.D. Cooper towering over the others.

He released a breath and pulled the truck to a stop about twenty yards from the helicopter. Before he'd cut the engine, Megan had grabbed her duffel from the backseat and was out the door, jogging toward the helicopter.

It was the chance he'd been waiting for. She had everything she'd brought onto this journey with her. She was safely out the door, on her way to her cousins, who would protect her with their lives.

It was time.

He watched her longer than he should have, unable to drag his gaze from her trim figure, the waves of auburn hair shining like molten copper in the morning sunlight.

She wouldn't understand his choice. He wouldn't, if he were in her position.

He closed his eyes. Took a deep breath.

Then he turned the key in the ignition and jammed the truck in Reverse, peeling back out of the gate and onto the access road, raising a cloud of dust that mercifully hid Megan and her cousins from his rearview mirror.

He pulled out the cell phone and pushed the speed dial button he'd set up last night before going to bed.

Major Gantry answered on the first ring, sounding as if he hadn't slept all night. "Are you in North Carolina yet?"

"Nearly." Out of caution, he hadn't told Gantry anything about Megan being with him or their planned stop in Wytheville. It was vital that she get away cleanly.

"How long will it take for you to get to our meeting place?" Gantry's tight voice was starting to make Evan's shoulder muscles bunch in sympathy.

"Another hour. Maybe a little longer." He checked the rearview mirror again, half expecting to see

Megan racing down the road after him, gunning for his blood. But the road was, so far, empty of vehicles in both directions.

"You haven't told anyone where you're going, have you?"

"No," he said. As far as Megan and her cousins knew, he was headed to Fort Bragg in Fayetteville. "What about you?"

"Are you crazy?"

It wasn't a particularly comforting reply, but it would have to do, Evan thought. "Do you really have information about Vince Randall's death, or are you just running me around North Carolina for no good reason?"

"I do. I have everything you want to know and more."

The farther he got from Megan, the more the doubts began to creep past his resolve, twisting around his conscience like a kudzu vine. "How do you know what I want to know?"

"You think what goes on at the Pentagon doesn't trickle down to the officers? I know your suspicions. The questions you've been asking haven't exactly endeared me to my superiors."

"You got a promotion."

"I got shot to get that." For the first time on this call, Elmore Gantry sounded like the fiery young captain Evan remembered. "Just meet me in an hour where I told you to go. I'll answer all your questions then." Gantry hung up the phone.

Evan gazed forward, his gut aching. He was taking a huge risk, going alone to meet Gantry. Especially since he'd just left behind four able-bodied Cooper men and a tough as nails Cooper woman who had even more incentive than he did to get to the truth about Vince Randall's death.

It had seemed the thing to do just five minutes ago, but now it just looked like a stupid decision. *What are you really running away from, Pike?*

STARING OPEN-MOUTHED AT the pickup truck disappearing in a cloud of dust, Megan had absolutely no idea how to feel. Angry? As a wet hen. Hurt? Like she'd just been kicked in the stomach. Betrayed?

Yeah. She felt betrayed.

"Um, is that—"

She looked up at her cousin Gabe, trying not to cry. "He just ditched us."

"Why would he do that?"

The only reason she could think of, the only one that made any sense, was that he wanted to keep her out of any potential ambush he might be heading into. Which was utterly stupid, because if he was actually heading into an ambush, he was doing it alone, without the aid of her big, strapping cousins, including a former marine major and a navy chopper pilot roughly the size of a grizzly bear.

Would he really take such a risky chance just to keep her out of danger?

Yes, he would, her heart told her, and she felt some of her anger melting away.

Some of it. Not all of it.

Because there was also a pretty good chance that he had fled to keep from dealing with the attraction that kept cropping up between them no matter how hard they both tried to ignore it.

Maybe he'd just ditched her to keep from having to deal with her.

"What do you want to do?" J.D. asked, his blue eyes gentle. "We're gassed up and ready to fly. We can go back home if you want us to. Or do we go after him?"

"We have to go after him," she said flatly. "He could be heading into an ambush alone, the idiot." *And if anyone is going to kill him,* she added silently, *it's going to be me.*

"You think he's still headed to Fayetteville?" J.D. asked as they got into the Bell 206L.

She thought about it for a second as she settled into the forward facing seat near the back. "No," she said finally. "But he thinks that's where we'll think he's going."

Gabe arched his eyebrows. "That's mighty convoluted."

"Yeah, well, that appears to be how he thinks."

"We could try to spot him from the air," J.D. suggested, settling in the cockpit. Luke sat in the seat next to her, while Gabe and Jake sat in the seats facing them.

"Does Shane's truck have a GPS tracker in it?" she asked J.D., getting angry all over again. Evan had not only ditched her. He'd ditched her in a truck they'd borrowed from her cousin's good-natured new boyfriend.

"Probably not. I can call Cissy and find out—"

Gabe's cell phone rang. He looked at the display. "Alicia." He answered. "Hey, there. What's up?"

As Gabe listened to whatever his wife was telling him, Megan felt something digging into her hip. Shifting, she pulled out the offending cell phone, gazing at the darkened display.

If she called Evan, would he answer?

"I'll tell them," Gabe said and closed the phone. Megan could tell from his grim look that whatever he'd learned, it was bad. "Alicia was doing some digging for your brother—about this Major Gantry. She came across some details about his tour of duty in Kaziristan four years ago when Vince was killed. Turns out he had a special duty while he was there."

"What?" she asked.

"Liaison with MacLear Security."

Megan's gut rolled. "So he could be in the SSU's pocket."

Next to her, Luke spat a fierce profanity. Luke had experienced the ruthlessness of the SSU personally, when Barton Reid had sent his private army of thugs after Abby Chandler, going so far as to threaten her two-year-old son's life in order to get her to cooperate.

A two-year-old who turned out to be Luke's son, as well.

The ordeal may have brought Abby, Luke and little Stevie together as a family, but not before SSU agents had kidnapped the little boy and nearly gotten him killed.

As far as Luke was concerned, Megan knew, Barton Reid and the SSU had to go down. As soon and as permanently as possible.

And Evan Pike believed he was going to see the man who could make that happen. Had he already made different arrangements to meet Major Gantry?

Was he driving straight into an ambush?

"Would Evan know about Gantry's connection to MacLear?" she asked aloud.

Gabe shook his head. "Alicia said it wasn't widely known beyond Gantry's superiors. Apparently Gantry was specially requested by MacLear and didn't want it getting around the base in case his men thought he was choosing the private contractors' interests over theirs."

"But was he?" Megan asked, disturbed by the thought. Had he set up Vince's murder for MacLear?

She turned on the phone and tried Evan's cell number. As she had expected, the call went to voice mail.

"Evan, it's Megan. Don't hang up until you hear this. You have to call me back." She waved toward the helicopter's onboard satellite phone. Gabe read her the number and she repeated it over the cell phone, then continued. "Major Gantry was a special liaison to MacLear Security. They requested him specially for the job. I don't think he's on the up and up. If you're heading to meet him, don't do it. You could be walking into an—

The phone beeped. She'd exceeded the voice mail time limit.

"Ambush," she finished, her heart in her throat.

EVAN GLANCED AT THE CELL PHONE, wondering if he'd made yet another mistake by ignoring Megan's phone call. Though nearly an hour had passed since her call, he hadn't yet had the nerve to hear what she had to say.

But what if she and her cousins were in trouble? What if they needed his help?

With a growl of frustration, he grabbed the phone and checked for a voice mail. There it was, Megan's voice, low and intense as she told him about Elmore Gantry's connection to MacLear Security.

Which made Evan's decision to meet Gantry alone look even more stupid than it did already.

She'd left a phone number for him to call. She answered on the first ring, talking loud to be heard over the roar of the helicopter's engine. "Evan?"

"Are you in flight? You're not supposed to be on a cell—"

"This bird has a satellite air phone. Listen—"

"I have to meet him, Megan. This could be our best chance to get to the truth." Unless he was ambushed first.

"You're probably walking into an ambush." Megan sounded frantic with worry.

"Maybe. Probably," he conceded. "But I have to meet him. If I don't, everything we've gone through the past few days could be for nothing."

"Let us back you up," she pleaded.

He thought about it. Nothing had changed, really. His reasons for keeping her out of this mess remained.

But most of those reasons were selfish, weren't they? If their theories about MacLear were right, Gantry could have facilitated Vince's murder.

Megan deserved the chance to confront him, even if it was dangerous.

"Okay," he said. "I'm meeting Gantry east of Pilot Mountain, North Carolina. Near Flat Rock. Right now, I'm heading south on I-74. Think you can find me?"

There was a brief pause in which he could hear nothing over the roar of the helicopter engine. Then Megan was back. "Luke says we're about twenty minutes away. Keep heading there and we'll catch up. You'll hear us before we see you, so when you do, pull over on the shoulder and get out so we know it's you."

"Okay. See you soon." He hung up the phone and prayed he was doing the right thing.

Like it or not, he needed Megan with him. She seemed to fill up the holes in him, help him stay focused. He was stronger with her than without her.

But would it be enough to keep them both alive?

Chapter Sixteen

Megan peered through the port window of the Bell LongRanger, trying to pick out the black truck from the flow of interstate traffic a mile below. Suddenly, the helicopter swept right, taking them over a lush wooded area west of the highway. "Where are we going?" she said into the headset.

J.D. answered, his voice tinny through the earphones. "There's another bird in the area—we're getting too close."

"Do you have visual on the other bird?" Luke asked. Megan could hear his tense tone even over the speaker. She glanced at him and saw him peering through the windows, looking for the other helicopter.

"Not now, but I caught sight of it about a minute ago, heading south," J.D. answered. "Dark green Sikorsky. Probably an S-76."

"Does that mean anything to you?" Megan asked Luke, whose frown had deepened.

"That's what MacLear used. They sold off their assets after the company went down, but—"

Megan's gut clenched. "We need to let Evan know. What if he hears that helicopter and pulls over?"

"If that's the SSU out there, could they have picked up Megan's sat phone call?" Jake asked.

"I'm not sure anyone outside the NSA could at this point," Luke said. "It's worth risking a call to warn him."

Megan grabbed the satellite phone again and made the call. As soon as Evan answered, she told him about the other helicopter. "It may be nothing—"

"Or it may be the bad guys," Evan finished grimly. "Okay, the pulling over idea isn't going to work. I can't get a visual on it without running off the road."

"We proceed to the rendezvous," she said, her tone equally bleak. "J.D.'s already found us a place to set down—meet us there." She gave him directions. "We can scout out the location Gantry gave you to meet him."

"I should have let us surprise him in Fayetteville," Evan said. "I'm sorry. Calling him was a stupid move."

"It was," she agreed, keeping her tone soft. "I've made a few of those in my life. It happens. See you when you get there." She hung up the phone, struck by how bereft she felt without Evan's voice in her ear.

He'd become a fixture in her life. How had that happened?

"We'll be there in twenty minutes," J.D. said. "You might want to check your weapons now. Not sure what we'll run into once we touch down."

Trust J.D. to be the pragmatic one, Megan thought. The eldest of her cousins, he'd also been through hell and back more times than she wanted to think about. Losing his wife, nearly losing his son to a ruthless drug boss willing to use the boy to get his revenge on the Coopers—she supposed to J.D., dealing with a helicopter full of crooked mercenaries probably seemed more like a vacation.

She wished she could be as calm. By now, she was as convinced as Evan that the SSU had been behind her husband's murder. Someone—Gantry, maybe?—had made sure Barton Reid knew about what Vince had witnessed in Tablis. Knowing Vince, he'd probably even made a point to track Reid and his terrorist contact through Tablis, which explained why he'd been spending time in the capital in the days leading up to his death.

If the SSU would kill an American soldier in cold blood in the middle of a peacekeeping mission, what compunction would they have about killing a civilian in the middle of Nowhere, North Carolina?

"He's tougher than his civilian background would suggest, Megan." Luke spoke with gentle understanding. "I did a little looking into his background. He did some combat training before he went over to Kaziristan. He's also put in extra training time since—he was supposed to go over to Afghanistan with a Pentagon team right before he resigned from his job. My friend at the Pentagon said Pike took what he did pretty seriously. Turned out to be a damned good marksman."

She looked at Luke, managing a smile. "This your way of telling me he can take care of himself?"

"Nobody can really take care of himself," he answered. "But lucky for him, he has you. And you have us."

She reached over and squeezed his hand. "Have I told you lately how glad I am you finally got your backside home where you belong?"

He grinned at her. "Glad to be home."

The landing site was a relatively flat patch of farmland just east of Pilot Mountain. J.D.'s friend in Wytheville knew the land owner and had arranged things for J.D.

The farmer came out to meet them as soon as the blades stopped turning. He was younger than Megan expected, a hard-bodied man in his early thirties who introduced himself as Duncan McElroy. "Nice bird."

J.D. shook his hand and handled the introduction of the others. "Cody Bollinger said you might be able to transport us to Flat Rock."

McElroy nodded. "I've got a big Ford Explorer. I can take all of y'all where you want to go." He slanted a look at the bulge of their concealed weapons visible under their clothes. "I'm assuming, since I know Cody pretty well, that he didn't send a bunch of thugs down here for me to haul around. But for a bunch of day tourists, y'all sure are packing a lot of heat."

J.D. and the others looked at Megan, leaving it up to her how much to share with the farmer. J.D. seemed to trust Cody Bollinger. And Bollinger apparently trusted McElroy.

"We're expecting an ambush," she said aloud.

McElroy's brows ticked upward. "So why are you going?"

"Because someone murdered my husband four years ago and got away with it. And we think the person we're going to meet can tell us who and why."

McElroy gave her a thoughtful look. "Why aren't the cops involved in this, then?"

"Nobody else thinks it was murder."

"And you're sure it was?"

"Yes."

His eyes narrowed slightly, as if he was weighing what she'd told him against the risks of getting involved. "Where did the murder take place?"

"Kaziristan," she answered bluntly. "My husband was a sergeant in the army on a peacekeeping mission."

As she expected, his eyes narrowed farther. "And you're sure it's murder and not combat-related?"

She thought about Evan's conviction, about all they'd learned over the past few days, and nodded. "Positive."

He seemed to give it another few seconds of thought. "Okay. I'll take you. But I'm not dropping the bunch of you off to fend for yourselves in the middle of the woods. Let me fetch my rifle and I'll come with you."

"I'm not sure—" J.D. began.

McElroy stopped him with a fierce look. "I spent five years in the Marine Corps myself. I know what I'm doing and I damned well know those woods out there better than any of y'all." His expression softened to an almost boyish grin. "And frankly, farming ain't exactly the most exciting way to pass time. I could do with some mixing it up." His grin faded. "Suppose you'd better tell me what we're up against."

While J.D. explained the situation to McElroy, Megan walked away and pulled out her cell phone to call Evan.

He answered on the second ring. "You're on the ground?"

"Just a few minutes ago. We've picked up another warm body." She told him about Duncan McElroy. "He knows these woods, so we thought it would be best to bring him in."

"Does he know what he's getting into?"

"He's finding out." She looked over her shoulder.

McElroy hadn't started running yet, at least. "Have you heard any more from the other helicopter?"

"They flew south."

"Toward Pilot Mountain?"

"In that general direction."

They hadn't seen the helicopter again, but he could have passed too far north or south of their landing spot for them to be able to get another visual. "It could be a coincidence."

"You think?"

"No," she admitted. "Where are you now?"

"I'm off the interstate, heading east of Pilot Mountain. I'm passing through Flat Rock right now."

She was surprised. He must have made good time, or else their detours to avoid the other helicopter had slowed them down more than she realized, because he was a lot closer than she thought he'd be. "If you see anything hinky at all on the way here, get the hell out of there and call us for backup."

"Will do." He paused a second, then started again, his voice lower and more intimate. "Megan, about last night—" There was a shattering sound over the line, and his voice cut off abruptly.

Her heart jumped. "Evan?"

When he spoke again, he was out of breath. "Someone just shot out the back window. I think I've run into our ambush."

"Get out of there!"

"I'm trying! I may have to ditch the truck. I'm a smaller target on foot."

"You're safer in the truck!"

"I have to get off the phone. I'll call when I can." The line went dead.

Megan ran back to the others, her heart in her throat. "We have to go now! Evan's taking fire!"

EVAN SPOTTED A LARGE BLACK Hummer barreling up the two-lane road in front of him, and warning bells rang in his head immediately. On instinct, he whipped the truck off the road at the first turnoff into the dense woods and gunned it as fast as he dared up the dirt road, praying he wouldn't come across hikers or catch an ATV rider unaware.

Dust flew up behind his truck, hiding anything that might be coming behind him. But all his pursuers had to do was follow the dust cloud to find him.

He had to leave the truck and go on foot.

Back in Alabama, Megan had eluded their pursuers by taking unexpected turns at the last possible moment, but there were no easy turnoffs on this dirt track. In fact, he was terrified he was going to come to the end of the road any minute.

But as he heard the sound of vehicles gaining ground behind him, he saw his best chance—a grassy trail ahead to the left, just wide enough for the truck to handle, at least for a short way. He waited until the last moment and jerked the wheel to the left, fishtailing on the dirt road but somehow managing not to roll the truck. Dust clouds shot up behind him, and he used the cover to brake and slam the truck into Park. He rolled out the passenger side, using the truck for cover, and darted into the woods, zigzagging as they'd done during their race down Gossamer Mountain.

The trail was uphill most of the way, through dense scrubby underbrush on hard-packed, rocky soil. Ahead, a large boulder loomed out of the woods, providing natural cover he couldn't turn down. He bolted behind the outcropping and listened for sounds of pursuit.

He could hear them crashing about the woods, not even bothering with stealth. The Coopers had said the SSU agents had learned from their previous skirmishes to be prepared, but they weren't in Gossamer Ridge anymore, and Evan wasn't a Cooper. He had never been in this part of North Carolina before, and for all he knew, one of the men down there chasing him was a native.

His cell phone rang, making him jump. He jammed his hand into his pocket and put it on vibrate before he pulled it out of his jeans. Megan, of course.

"Bad timing," he answered in a whisper.

"Are you okay?" She sounded scared. He found comfort in her obvious concern for him, given how bone-headed his decisions had been over the past twenty-four hours. He wouldn't have blamed her if she'd hopped on that bird in Wytheville and headed back to Alabama. The last thing he'd wanted to do was cause Megan Randall more distress.

"I'm safe," he answered. "For now, anyway. But I had to ditch the truck."

"Damn it, I told you—"

"Trust me, I'm safer on foot."

She released a huff of frustration. "Where are you?"

"In the woods somewhere off Sweeney Road, east of Flat Rock. I turned to the right off on a dirt road about a mile east of three tall towers—maybe broadcast towers?"

He heard the muffled sound of Megan talking to someone else. "Any idea how many people are following you?"

"Two vehicles, at least. Whoever was shooting at me, plus a black Hummer coming from the opposite direction. How many in each vehicle, I'm not sure."

"Someone's bound to call the police if they hear gunshots," she murmured, sounding worried.

"They're using sound suppressors. I didn't hear a thing until the bullet hit my back window."

"Are you sure it was a bullet?"

"There's a big hole in the dashboard that says yes." He sneaked a peek around the boulder hiding him and spotted a man wearing old woodland camouflage, carrying an M-16 with a sophisticated-looking sound suppressor screwed onto the end of the barrel. His gut tightened.

The man started to turn toward the boulder. Evan hunkered down again, trying not to make a sound.

"Evan?" Megan's breathless query buzzed in his ear, but he couldn't answer. He listened to the sound of the man's footsteps crunching past him. So bold. Not even trying to be stealthy. Clearly confident that Evan couldn't get away.

There were houses somewhere over the hill. The area where he'd pulled off the road had been densely wooded, but it wasn't uninhabited. What would those camouflaged men do if they stumbled across some poor farmer or hiker in the woods?

He dared another quick look. The man had his back to Evan now, moving deeper into the woods. He topped the rise and disappeared down the other side.

"Evan!" Megan repeated.

"Sorry," he whispered into the phone. "Just had a close call. I'm hidden for now, but I don't know how long that's going to last."

"We need to get you out of there."

"I'll agree with that."

Her voice went muffled again, then came back clear and strong. "We're coming to get you."

"Not you." The words came out before he could stop them.

"Not up for a vote," she answered flatly. "My

cousins are going to draw them away from you. We've already figured out your position—"

"How?"

"The cell phones we borrowed came from Cooper Security, remember? They had trackers in them so Jesse could locate us in case we needed help. He just called with the coordinates."

"Son of a bitch." He didn't know whether to be pissed or relieved. "Just so I don't overreact to whatever y'all are going to be up to—what are y'all going to be up to?"

"Luke looks the most like you, size-wise and in general coloring, so he's going to try to draw them after him."

"That's crazy."

Megan sighed. "That's Luke."

He didn't want anyone else putting his neck on the line to save his skin. But he supposed Luke Cooper of all the Coopers had a bone to pick with the SSU. "Okay. But hurry."

"We're already on Sweeney Road, coming from the east," she told him. "I spotted one of the broadcast towers you were talking about just a minute ago. We're pulling over right now to let Luke get the show on the road."

This was insanity, Evan thought. But he was in no position to question whatever help he could get.

"Gabe and Jake are going to trail Luke in case he gets in trouble," Megan told Evan. "You still okay? Need to hang up and move to a new position?"

"I'm okay for now," he assured her, looking around for another place to hide if his position became compromised. About fifty yards away, a canopy of kudzu draped a couple of trees, offering a possible hiding place. Edging to the other side of the boulder, he took a quick peek. He saw two more men in camouflage, talking into shoulder-mounted radio receivers. Suddenly they bolted east. "Hmm, looks like the distraction ploy may be working."

"Great. I'll be with you in just a few minutes."

"Wait—what?"

But she'd hung up already.

He muttered a silent oath and flattened his back against the rock. Why the hell couldn't she be the "wait in the car" type of woman?

If she was, you wouldn't be falling in love with her, answered a voice in the back of his mind.

IT'S JUST LIKE THE WOODS *back home,* Megan told herself as she started hiking a circular route through the woods. She sneaked another quick look at the GPS map on her phone. She was still heading toward Evan's position, more slowly than she liked, perhaps, but she was closing in.

To the east, she heard distant rustling noises in the woods. She hoped it was coming from the SSU agents being lured away from Evan, but she couldn't be certain.

Ahead, she saw a canopy of kudzu draped like

a blanket over a pair of damaged trees. The leafy vines blocked her view of the hillside, forcing her to slow her forward movement. For all she knew, a couple of SSU agents were camped out on the other side, waiting in ambush.

J.D. and Duncan McElroy had both wanted to accompany her, but she'd refused their help. One person sneaking through the woods was going to be trouble enough to conceal. Two or three would almost certainly draw at least one or two SSU agents back toward Evan's position.

She edged forward, staying low, moving one silent step at a time toward the wall of kudzu. She was mostly camouflaged, having pulled on one of Vince's old camouflage-patterned T-shirts, the one she wore as a sleeping shirt. She'd covered her black jeans with dirt as soon as she exited McElroy's SUV, creating a more natural camouflage for her bottom half. Her red hair was tucked up tightly under a camouflage cap she'd borrowed from Jake, and her bare skin was dirt-dusted, too. Not perfect concealment for a stealthy approach, she supposed, but good enough in a pinch.

She was almost at the kudzu when she heard a snapping sound somewhere behind her. She froze in place, listening.

Suddenly, sound rushed toward her, rustling, crackling, like a whirlwind loosened in the woods only a couple of feet behind her. She reached to her hip for her Ruger, but it was too late. Steel-hard arms wrapped around her, crushing her back against a warm but rock-hard body. A hand clamped over her mouth, cutting off her gasp.

Please be Evan, she thought, her heart racing.

But her body told her the truth long before she heard the unfamiliar voice, low and harsh in her ear.

"Not a sound. They will hear you."

Her captor grabbed her gun from her holster and whipped her around to face him, holding her wrist to keep her from running. Haggard gray eyes met hers, dark with desperation. She recognized the lean features, though the lines and creases in his face were deeper and there was no sign of the smile he'd worn in the photo that even now sat tucked inside her wallet. Snapped a few weeks before his death, the photo depicted Vince, his unit, and their captain, Elmore Gantry.

The same Elmore Gantry who now stood before her, holding her gun in one hand and her life in the other.

Chapter Seventeen

"Don't make a sound."

Gantry's whisper buzzed in Megan's ears as she tried to focus her scattered wits enough to make the right choice. He had her gun but not her cell phone. If she could lead him away from Evan's position—

"You know who I am, don't you?" he asked, his voice barely audible.

She nodded, willing her pulse down to a bearable rhythm. "You set us up."

"Not on purpose," he said. "Where is he?"

"I'm not telling you that."

"I have to find him before they do."

"They? Who's they?" She knew the answer, of course, was more convinced than ever that former MacLear SSU mercenaries had been hired by someone—most likely Barton Reid—to systematically erase all the evidence of his crimes. But she wanted to hear Gantry admit the truth himself.

"Barton Reid has rehired elements who had earlier worked for MacLear Security. I'm sure you know all about them—your brother was a MacLear agent."

"He never worked for Barton Reid."

"Good for him." Gantry's tone was bleak. "I can help Pike, but you have to get me to him."

"You've found me."

Megan whirled around to see Evan move out from behind the canopy of kudzu, his pistol leveled with Gantry's head. She jerked her hand away from Gantry's grip before he could react and moved out of Evan's line of fire.

Gantry held up both hands. "I'm not here to hurt anyone."

"Drop the weapon. Kick it over to Megan."

"We can't play these games—there's no time!" But Gantry did as Evan asked, lowering the Ruger to the ground and sliding it through the underbrush toward her.

Megan bent to pick it up and heard a thud and a loud grunt. Gantry pitched forward into her, knocking her to the ground.

She gripped her Ruger and stared at Gantry, who lay half atop her, his eyes wide with pain.

"Stay down!" Evan growled, crawling toward her on his hands and knees. He crouched behind her, guarding her body with his.

"He's been shot," Megan hissed, seeing frothy blood bubbling around Gantry's lips.

"That was sniper fire," Evan said, his voice tight. "We've got to find cover—now!" He tried to pull her to her feet, but she resisted, holding on to Gantry's arms.

"We can't leave him here—"

"He made his own choice. He got what he deserved."

"Reid—" Gantry gasped. "He made me do it—"

"He can testify against Barton Reid," Megan said fiercely. "He can put that bastard away. We can't leave him to his fate. He could be dying!"

Evan gave a low growl of frustration and pulled her up. "You stay low. Go over the rise and find us cover. I'll bring Gantry with me."

"Put me over your back." Gantry's voice was thready, tight as if he were struggling for air, but the blood around his mouth wasn't any worse— perhaps he'd simply bitten his tongue?

"You can't walk at all?" Evan asked.

"Put me over your back—body armor—"

Evan exchanged a glance with Megan before looking back at Gantry. "Are you even hurt?" he asked the man.

"I think the impact broke a rib—maybe pierced— lung—"

"Put him over your back," Megan said. "See you on the other side." She didn't waste a second, springing up the incline, haphazardly changing her direction as she ran. She heard a bullet whistle past once, making her stutter-step, but she kept going, not looking back, until she had topped the crest and was scrambling down the other side.

Ahead she saw a grouping of boulders that could give them cover. She raced toward it, ducking behind the larger of the four rocks. Hearing the sound of rocks and dirt tumbling down the mountainside, she risked a quick peek and saw Evan sliding down the incline, dragging Major Gantry behind him.

She waved her hand at him, hoping he could see, for she didn't dare risk calling out. He gave a wave back and somehow kept his footing long enough to join her behind the boulder, pulling Gantry to the safety of cover.

The major was as pale as milk, his lips turning a scary-looking gray. The odd sucking sound he made when he breathed made Megan's heart tumble. "He looks terrible," she murmured to Evan, reaching down to Gantry's throat to check his carotid pulse. It was fast and thready.

"I think he was right about puncturing his lung," Evan replied, scanning the area around them for an impending ambush.

"Then we have to get him out of here." She looked up at Evan. "Alive. He said he'd testify against Barton Reid."

"I guess we'd better put out an SOS call to your cousins, then, because they've got us pretty well pinned down."

"The road—" Gantry's voice was a guttural groan.

"What about the road?" Evan asked.

"There's—a road—down the mountain. Two or three miles."

Megan peered through the dense woods below, looking for any sign of a road. She thought she saw a flicker of movement, a spot of color that might have been a vehicle passing along a mostly hidden road. "I don't know if we can drag him down there ourselves without hurting him more—" Megan's cell phone vibrated. She reached into her jeans pocket and checked it. "Text from Luke—the SSU operatives seem to be retreating."

"You think they believe Gantry's dead?"

She looked at the hole in Gantry's shirt. Straight to the heart. "If he weren't wearing body armor, he *would* be dead."

If Vince had been wearing body armor, would he have survived the sniper shot that took him down?

Why hadn't he been wearing armor?

She looked up at Evan. "I can't believe I never asked anyone this question before. Why wasn't Vince wearing body armor on patrol?"

He sighed. "It was a hundred degrees in the shade, and we hadn't had any combat action in almost two weeks. Things had calmed down in our sector. Nobody was expecting sniper fire."

"I told them they didn't have to," Gantry said.

Megan's chest hurt. She grabbed the front of Gantry's shirt, making him grunt in pain. "Did you know someone was going to shoot him?"

"Megan—" Evan caught her arms and pulled

her away from Gantry. "You're going to hurt him worse."

Rage churned in her belly, waves of hot nausea threatening to spill over. She fought for control, knowing deep down that she had to stay focused or they'd all be killed.

"Did you know?" she asked Gantry again, keeping her tone low and calm. Evan's grip on her arms loosened.

"I didn't know. Not until—after." Gantry groped for her hand. Finding it, he squeezed weakly. "If I'd known, I wouldn't have let it happen."

She pulled her hand away and turned to Evan. "Can you get to the road?"

He nodded, watching her carefully. "He can testify against Reid if he lives."

She knew a warning when she heard one. Apparently, he thought if he left her alone with Gantry, she just might do the man in. Hell, maybe she would. Not on purpose, but right now, anger chafed inside her like a chained tiger. She had to get it under control. Their lives might depend on it.

"He'll be alive when you get back with help," she promised.

Evan touched her cheek, his palm rough and warm. "Are you a good shot?" he asked, edging closer to her until she thought he was about to kiss her.

"Pretty good."

"You may have to give me cover fire, so try not

to use up your ammo." He pressed his lips to her brow. "Shoot for the throat if it comes to that—they're wearing body armor, too."

Then he was off, running a crooked pattern down the mountainside toward the road below.

Megan watched the ridge for any sign of gunmen, but there was nothing. She pulled out her cell phone to let her cousins know where they could find Evan and discovered another text from Luke. She hadn't even noticed the vibration in the chaos. "All vehicles gone from woods except Shane's truck. Tires flat."

A preventive measure to keep Evan from doubling back and escaping? Or had it been a petty final salute before they bugged out? Megan wasn't sure it mattered.

She texted back the information about Evan and requested a 911 call to authorities, as well—Major Gantry was injured. She pocketed the phone again and looked at Gantry. He wasn't any better, but he didn't look that much worse, either.

He was gazing back at her with solemn gray eyes. "I'm sorry. I really am."

"For what? Getting my husband killed? Or getting caught?"

"I covered it up. I didn't cause it." His breathing was a little better, she noticed—maybe he didn't have a collapsed lung after all. But then he gave a long, rattling wheeze with his next breath and she went back to being afraid he was going to die before help arrived. She might have only a little time to get the answers she needed.

"Why did you cover it up? Were you involved in the SSU scandal? Were you working with Barton Reid?"

"Not with him—" Gantry's wheeze intensified. "He had something on my wife."

"Your wife?"

"We were having trouble with finances. While I was gone, she took money. From her company."

Embezzlement. "And Barton Reid knew about it?"

"He knows everything about everyone." He tried a shallow cough and grimaced with agony. "Makes it a point."

"He blackmailed you into covering up Vince's death?"

Gantry nodded. "She'd put the money back—nobody knew except us and the junior partner of the firm. But somehow, Reid found out. He threatened to tell the senior partner. She'd lose her job, probably go to jail—" His anguished expression tugged at her heart. "My kids are four and seven. I'm gone all the time—they barely know me—"

"All you had to do was go along with the official story about Vince's death?"

"And not tell anyone I saw Barton Reid with Malik Tahrim."

"He's a terrorist?"

"Al Adar connected—bad news."

"You'll testify to all of this?"

Gantry nodded again. "I was wrong to sit on it. My marriage is crumbling because of the pressure. My wife and I can't even look at each other—"

"The truth will set you free," she murmured.

"Or get you killed."

The wry tone of the masculine voice behind her sent a shiver down her spine as she whirled to face the camouflage-clad man standing behind her, his rifle pointed at her chest.

HALFWAY DOWN THE MOUNTAIN, Evan's cell phone buzzed. He took cover behind a tree and checked the phone. There was a text message from Jesse Cooper. He read the message twice to be sure he was seeing what he thought.

His blood ran cold.

He peered up the mountain toward the boulders where he'd left Megan and Elmore Gantry and spotted a man in camouflage creeping up the hill. Even from this distance, Evan should have been able to hear him moving through the underbrush, but the man in camouflage walked with the practiced stealth of a hunter.

He was lean, tall, but not imposing. Young—mid-twenties, maybe. Like most of the other SSU agents, trained by former military instructors at MacLear, this man had the poise and bearing of a soldier.

Remembering the message he'd just received

from Jesse Cooper, Evan knew exactly who the man in camouflage had to be. And he was heading straight toward the boulders where Megan and Gantry were hunkered down.

There was no time to lose. The decision was made—the woman he loved was up there, vulnerable, with no idea that death was heading her way.

No idea that death wore the face of someone she thought she could trust.

Sliding his P32 from his ankle holster, he headed up the mountain after the stalker.

IT TOOK A FEW SECONDS for Megan to look away from the barrel of the M6 rifle long enough to meet the intruder's clear gray eyes, seconds that could have meant the end of her life if he'd wanted to shoot her.

But he didn't. "I'm not here to kill *you*."

"You're here to kill him?"

"What do you care? He lied to you for years." With a little flick of the gun barrel, he indicated he wanted her out of his way. She realized her body was blocking his shot at Gantry, who lay wedged behind her against the rocks.

"And you're trying to keep the cover-up going," she retorted, wondering if she could move fast enough to push the barrel up and away before he could get a shot off.

Probably not, she decided.

"You think there aren't people in every government in every country making messy decisions?"

"And that makes it okay?"

"I'm sayin' they're all alike. You just have to figure out how you can get your piece of it."

A hint of a Southern drawl slipped out, and she realized she knew his voice. It took a second to place it, but when it did, her gut tightened painfully. "You son of a bitch."

His eyes narrowed.

"Yes, I know who you are," she growled. "Shane Mason."

With a sigh, he pulled down the green balaclava covering the bottom half of his face. "It was just a job."

"You were messing with my cousin, who happens to have had enough crap to deal with in her life— Wait! You started dating her two months ago! Were you an SSU agent the whole time?"

"We're not the SSU," he protested, looking angry. "We don't belong to anyone but ourselves."

"Looks like you belong to Barton Reid to me," she said. "Bought and paid for."

A pained look creased his face, as if her words had hit the mark. "Please move out of my way. I'm not here to hurt you. I never was."

"No, you're here to shoot an injured man in cold blood."

"He betrayed us."

"He betrayed Barton Reid," she shot back. "And Barton Reid betrayed his country."

"The country betrayed him—betrayed us—a long time ago."

Megan stared at him, feeling as if the world had just upended beneath her feet. She'd known Shane Mason for two months—casually, but they'd run into each other more than once because of her cousin Cissy—and not once had he ever seemed remotely political. Yet the young man standing before her glowed with the fervor of a true believer.

"Is Shane Mason even your name?"

His only answer was to point the barrel of the M16 at her chest again. "I will shoot through you if I have to."

A sudden flicker of movement in the woods behind Mason caught her eye. She saw a flash of green-and-gray plaid, and her heart skipped a beat.

Evan had come back.

"I mean it, Megan. Move out of the way."

She stood her ground, forcing her gaze up to meet his. "You were in the army." She felt a flutter of pain in the center of her chest. "You told Cissy you'd been in Afghanistan, but that's not where you were, was it? You were in Kaziristan."

"Merriwether," Gantry murmured behind her. "His real name is Scott—Merriwether."

"Merriwether?" Chill bumps rose up Megan's arms. "I guess you didn't die in a car crash after all, huh? What did you do, grab some poor guy off the street, liquor him up and put him behind the wheel of your car? How'd you manage the DNA match?"

He smiled. "Nobody died. It was a cover story all along."

She narrowed her eyes. "The SSU has that kind of clout?"

"I told you, we're not the SSU."

"Then who are you?"

"Patriots."

"I don't think that means what you think it does."

"I suppose you think patriotism means a bunch of pampered middle-class idiots marching around talking about the founding fathers and balanced budgets and supporting the troops?" Mason—Merriwether, she corrected mentally—shook his head. "They send the troops out to protect their gold and their oil—they don't care about the troops."

"And Barton Reid does?"

Merriwether's smile made her gut clench. "Reid is just the tip of the iceberg."

So far, Scott Merriwether hadn't fired his rifle, despite how bloody long it had taken Evan to sneak back up the hill behind him. He was talking to Megan, his voice a low rumble that Evan couldn't quite discern from his position thirty yards away. He needed to be a lot closer if he wanted to get a decent shot. His Kel-Tec P32 had excellent accuracy, but nobody was a good shot with a pistol at thirty yards.

There was little cover if he wanted to go straight at the rifleman. He'd have to circle behind, which would eat up extra time. Looking at the rifle barrel pointed right at Megan's chest, he didn't know if he had extra time.

His heart was still racing like a hunted rabbit, as it had been ever since he'd read Jesse Cooper's text message.

"Merriwether isn't dead. Merriwether is Shane Mason."

No wonder the SSU had found them. They'd probably been tracking him and Megan through Merriwether's truck from the beginning.

Evan edged left, keeping low, hiding behind the cover of rocks and bushes. He'd lucked out in his choice of clothes for the day, a dark green and gray plaid shirt over a charcoal gray T-shirt that offered him more camouflage than he might have otherwise hoped for. He scooted in a looping circle until he was positioned about ten yards behind the man with the rifle.

From there, he saw the unmistakable outline of a bullet-resistant vest beneath the man's camo-patterned clothing. Muttering a low curse, he lifted his pistol sights to the back of the gunman's unprotected neck.

"Reid was always working for someone else," Merriwether said. "We all are."

"Someone in the government?" Megan asked.

"You have to work from inside out to create real change."

"What's your vision of America after the change?" Megan's voice was tight with tension, but Evan had to give her credit for remaining calm and focused, trying to draw Merriwether out and keep him talking.

If he weren't already completely mad about her, he'd have fallen a little in love with her just for that grace under fire.

"No more pretending we're saints, to begin with," Merriwether answered. "No more propping up dictators just because they'll happily take our money for their oil."

"Did you shoot Vince?"

Merriwether didn't answer Megan's low question.

She took a step closer to him, until her chest was inches from the M16's deadly barrel. Evan's breath caught in his throat, trapped by terror as the former soldier's finger twitched on the trigger.

"Did you kill my husband?" Her eyes blazed with fury.

Merriwether dropped the barrel of the M16, just a little.

"Why?" Megan's voice held so much hurt, it made Evan's heart ache for her. "Just because he saw Barton Reid with a terrorist? Just because he was in the wrong place at the wrong time, he had to die?"

Merriwether's back straightened as she took another step forward. He whipped the barrel of the rifle up again, and Evan knew, down to his marrow, that Merriwether was about to fire.

But as he raised the Kel-Tec to fire, the crack of a gunshot split the air.

Chapter Eighteen

A half dozen things seemed to happen all at once within the next few seconds of Megan's life. A flash of movement in the woods. The glint of sunlight on the M16 barrel as Merriwether swung it toward her. The leap of the Ruger in her hand as she squeezed the trigger. The deafening crack of gunfire.

She flung herself backward against the boulders as the barrel of the M16 continued an upward arc, even as Merriwether started to fall. With its strange, blatting noise, the sound-suppressed M16 sprayed bullets into the woods behind her, falling silent as Merriwether finally hit the ground.

She lay still, afraid to move. Afraid she'd sit up to find herself mortally wounded by a stray bullet. Afraid the flash of movement in the woods hadn't been Evan but one of Merriwether's accomplices, come to clean up the mess they'd left behind.

She felt something hot and wet move across her hand. Opening her eyes, she saw that Merriwether had fallen only a couple of feet away from her, blood from his ruined throat pouring into the ground as his heart pumped a few last, sporadic beats before he died.

She pulled her hand away from the blood and closed her eyes again, nausea rising in her throat.

"Megan?" Evan's voice. Faint. Scared.

She forced her eyes open and met his anguished gaze. "I'm okay," she said aloud, although she wasn't. She felt as sick as she'd ever remembered being, now that the adrenaline rush of the last few minutes was fading.

He knelt beside her, touching her face, but she pushed him away, scrambling on hands and knees a few feet away so she could empty her stomach without contaminating the crime scene.

She groaned as the dry heaves hit her, shuddering as Evan's hand smoothed over her back, comforting and humiliating at the same time. "I'm sorry," she gasped.

He pulled her hair away from her face. "Are you hurt?"

She shook her head, swallowing hard to fight the heaves. "Why'd you come back?"

"Jesse sent me a text—told me Merriwether was Shane Mason," Evan murmured.

She rubbed her aching eyes. "I guess he didn't die in a crash, after all."

"How did he fake his death? Did he say?"

"He said someone handled it. I'm not sure what that means," she admitted. She looked over at Merriwether's body. "Oh my God, what are we going to tell Cissy?"

The phone in her pocket vibrated. She sat back on her heels and checked the message. "J.D.'s still looking for you. You never showed up." She looked up at him, the fire in his gaze catching her off guard. "Evan?"

He reached out to touch her face, his hand trembling. In a sudden crush, he pulled her to him, pressing his face into her hair. They clung to each other for a long moment, until a rattling cough from behind her drew their attention to Major Gantry. He shot them an apologetic look as they pushed apart and scrambled to where he lay.

"I really think I need a hospital," he rasped.

Megan opened her phone to send an SOS to her cousins, but a new text message popped up before she could. Called in the Mounties. Help's on the way.

In the distance, Megan heard the first wail of sirens. She looked at Evan, who managed a faint smile.

"Boy, are we going to have a lot to explain," he said.

Megan slumped wearily next to Gantry, too numb to care.

THE NORTH CAROLINA AUTHORITIES weren't thrilled to hear about a gun battle in the middle of the woods, but eventually they sorted out the hunters from the hunted. By the time Evan was finally released after hours of exhausting interrogation, cool, blue night was falling across the Carolina hills.

Megan was nowhere in sight, but one of her cousins—either Jake or Gabe—sat in a chair in the waiting area near the police station's front desk. He looked up at Evan as he approached.

"No cuffs," he said bluntly. "I guess that's a good sign."

Evan sat in the chair next to him. "Have you heard anything from Megan?"

Gabe—or Jake—shook his head. "J.D. and Luke are still back there, too. Jake was released before I was—he's gone to see if he can find us something to eat."

So he was Gabe. "Any word about the guys who got away?"

Gabe shook his head. "We saw a Sikorsky take off not long after the dudes in camo bugged out, so we think they're probably long gone to wherever they came from."

Footsteps coming down the corridor toward them drew Evan's gaze upward. His heart leapt at the sight of Megan's pale, weary face. She was accompanied by Sergeant Blalock, one of the detectives who'd arrived on the scene just after an ambulance scooped up Gantry and headed for Wake Forest Baptist's trauma center.

Blalock looked angry. Fortunately, his ire didn't seem to be directed at Megan. "We'll comb this state 'til we find those squirrely bastards."

While he appreciated the sentiment, Evan was pretty sure their camo-clad friends were long gone by now. He focused his attention on Megan instead, searching her face for clues to how she was faring.

She looked tired. Still a little green around the gills, and he knew that might last a while. It didn't matter that Merriwether had been trying to shoot her. It didn't even matter that he was almost certainly the man who shot Vince Randall.

She'd killed a man today. That fact would haunt her for a long while.

She glanced his way, then looked away again, her expression shuttered. "Are we okay to leave now?" she asked the detective.

Blalock looked pained as he said, "Yeah. I reckon you are. We have your statements and your stories all check out." His expression shifted. "I guess once we heard the name Cooper, we should have figured out what was going on." At her arched eyebrow, he smiled. "You think two showdowns with the Cordero drug cartel don't make the news up here in the hills? Hell, I went in there and shook Luke Cooper's hand myself. Damned near asked for his autograph."

Luke Cooper himself emerged from a door half-way down the hallway, looking grim. He spotted them up the corridor and headed their way, another detective close on his heels.

"Are we done here?" he asked impatiently.

"Yes, sir, you are," Blalock answered.

"Where's J.D.?" he asked.

"He's talking to Duncan McElroy," Megan answered. "We need to get to the hospital—if anyone finds out where Gantry is—"

"I sent two of my men to guard him," Blalock interjected.

Evan wasn't sure that would be enough. "Is there somewhere we can shower around here?" He didn't want to barge into the hospital in sweaty, grimy clothes. Someone had retrieved his bag from the cab of the borrowed pickup truck and given it back to him right before he was cut loose, so he had a clean change of clothes. All he needed was some hot water and a bar of soap.

Blalock looked them over. "Yeah, I reckon y'all might want to scrape some of that mud off. I'll see what we can do."

He eventually pointed the men to communal showers near the officers' locker rooms and handed

Megan off to a female officer. Megan looked over her shoulder as she walked away, locking eyes with Evan briefly before she rounded the corner.

He watched her go, tamping down frustration. He had a feeling he wasn't going to get a second alone with Megan as long as her cousins were around.

By the time Duncan McElroy dropped them off at the hospital, Gantry was out of surgery to repair his nicked lung and was resting comfortably in ICU for the night. Two armed guards flanked his doorway, looking deadly serious about keeping him safe. But Megan knew Barton Reid and his hired killers were sophisticated enough to get past almost any level of security the local cops could provide.

Luke and J.D. talked to the police officers and the nurses, and, after one of the guards spoke to someone on the phone, the two Coopers entered Gantry's room. "They're better guards for him," Jake murmured to Megan, nudging her around the corner into the corridor. "They know what to look for."

"He needs to be deposed as soon as possible," Megan said. "Get it on tape. Witnessed and signed off—"

"In case he ends up mysteriously dead?" Gabe asked from her other side.

She looked at him. "Shh. His wife's probably right inside that waiting room."

She, Evan, and her cousins entered and found a small room furnished with comfortable-looking chairs and sofas. There were a handful of people scattered about the room, but it was easy to pick out Gantry's wife. She was a pretty woman with curly dark hair and tear-stained eyes who sat on one of the sofas, her arms wrapped around a couple of sleeping children.

She saw them coming and her eyes widened. "He said you'd be here. I just figured it would be morning."

"You spoke to him?" Megan pulled up a nearby chair and sat across from her. "How's he doing?"

"Better now, from what the doctors tell me." She looked scared but hopeful. "I don't even want to think what would have happened if he hadn't been w-wearing body armor."

"Did he tell you what he was doing?"

She nodded, shame burning in her eyes. "It's all my fault. I p-put him in this position—"

"Barton Reid put him in this position," Megan said firmly. "He has to pay. You understand that, don't you?"

"Yes." Her lip trembled but she lifted her head and nodded. "I do understand that. I have to deal with the consequences."

"We'll figure out a way to help you with that,

too." Evan pulled up a chair next to Megan and leaned forward, his expression fierce. "I'm a lawyer. I can help you find good representation."

"I've already told the senior partner what I did." She managed a bleak smile. "He's agreed not to press charges, since the money was returned with interest. But he's letting me go and he's not inclined to give me a good reference."

"That's something you can work with, isn't it?" Megan asked, sliding a quick look at Evan. She hadn't spoken two words to him since they'd left the woods, and even now, she didn't know what to say.

The last few days were a blur. It almost seemed like another woman's life, a woman she didn't recognize at all. Megan Cooper Randall didn't run for her life. She didn't hide out in Kentucky motels or hike through the woods evading camouflage-clad mercenaries carrying M16 rifles. She didn't shoot people to keep them from shooting her first.

She didn't fall in love with a man she'd spent the last four years blaming for her husband's death.

Her breath caught with dismay. Had she lost her mind?

Evan looked at her oddly, his expression full of heat. She felt an answering fire in the center of her chest and had to look away to keep her wits intact.

"You're really worried about his safety, aren't you?" Mrs. Gantry asked.

"We're going to do what we can to protect him," Megan promised. "My family—it's what we do."

She realized she hadn't checked in with any of her brothers or sisters in hours. She gave Mrs. Gantry's hand a gentle squeeze and stood, crossing to where Jake and Gabe sat near the door. She settled next to Gabe. "Have you talked to Jesse or any of the others? Are they still under surveillance?"

"Talked to him while I was out looking for food," Jake answered. "Their visitors have disappeared into the woodwork."

"I wonder if that's a good thing or a bad thing," she said.

"Not sure it's either." Evan dropped into the chair next to her. His shoulder brushed hers, and she felt an answering quiver low in her belly. "The one thing we know about the SSU is that they're in it for the money. It's why they were recruited in the first place."

"But from what we know of Merriwether, he was a true believer," Megan countered. "How do we know there aren't more of them out there?"

"That's why J.D. and Luke are in there guarding your Major Gantry," Gabe said. "But it doesn't follow that they'll come after us now. Even true believers pick their battles."

"What is it about Barton Reid that would suck in a kid like Merriwether?" she wondered aloud.

"The idea that there's a better way of life than

what we're living now, I guess," Evan answered. He pinned his intense gaze on her again, sending another tremor rumbling through her. "We'd all like to think there's something better out there."

Jake stood up. "I'm going to head outside and give Jesse another call, see if there's any news."

Gabe joined him. "I'd better give Alicia a call, too. She was already ticked off at being left behind." He followed his brother out, leaving Megan and Evan alone, finally.

Neither spoke for a few moments, the silence between them growing tense, until Megan could bear it no longer. "I guess I should thank you."

"For what?"

She met his curious gaze. "For making me listen to you. When you first came to Gossamer Ridge. I didn't want to hear what you had to say, but you wouldn't take no for an answer. Thank you for not giving up on Vince. You were right. He deserved justice."

"I hope he gets it." Evan's brow furrowed. "I hope it helps you, too. I know how much you miss him."

"I do." She saw a hint of dismay in his expression at her admission. "I'll always miss him."

"I know." He looked down at his hands.

"But I think I can let him go now."

His gaze snapped up again. "Are you sure?"

"I've had dreams of him, ever since he died." She smiled at the memory of the comfort those dreams had brought her. "Lately, he's been trying to convince me it's time to move on."

"You really think it's him?" There was no skepticism in his question, only curiosity.

She met his gaze. "I think it is. And he's right. He's dead. I'm not. I have to let go and move on with my life."

"That must be painful to think about." His gentleness brought tears to her eyes.

She fought them back. "Not as much as I expected."

He took a deep breath. "Look, I know this is terrible timing and really the wrong place—"

The look he gave her when he brought his gaze up to meet hers made her breath catch. His eyes blazed with miserable passion, terrible need.

"I don't think I can just walk away from you, Megan."

She blinked back more tears, terrified and overjoyed at the same time. "Good. I think."

He quirked an eyebrow. "You think?"

"I've loved only one man in my life before now."

"Before now?"

The giddy hope in his expression made her heart hurt. "I don't know how to date or be in a real relationship," she warned, feeling completely out of her element. "I'm probably going to be terrible at it. I wasn't very good at it the first time—I got really lucky that Vince was the forgiving sort."

He clasped her hands tightly in his, joy rising in

his eyes. "I don't need you to be good at anything. I don't need you to *do* anything. I just need you to be you."

Well, hell. There went the tears, burning down her cheeks before she could get them under control. She couldn't help but laugh softly at the look of worry on his face.

"I can do that," she said. "I can definitely be me."

He brought her hands to his mouth and kissed her knuckles. "Are you sure this is what *you* want?"

"Yes," she said quickly, before either of them could let creeping doubt get in the way.

He kissed her knuckles again. "Good."

"So, how are we going to do this? Am I supposed to move to North Carolina or something?" The doubts she'd been holding at bay began to slither back. She beat them back with ruthless determination. She would move, if that's what it took. As much as she loved her home, her family and her beloved Chickasaw County, she was done with long-distance relationships.

If Evan wanted her to be where he was, she'd go. She had to give this magic between them a chance to flourish.

"There's really nothing keeping me in North Carolina now, is there? I can take the bar exam anywhere."

"We could go to Kentucky," she offered. "You

might be able to see the place with new eyes now that you're older—"

He shook his head. "I do see it differently. But it's not my home anymore." He slid his arm around her shoulders, drawing her closer. "I thought I'd talk to Jesse about working at Cooper Security. I could be an asset to the legal department—"

"You could," she agreed quickly. "And I could put in a good word—I have clout there, you know."

He laughed softly. "I guess I should warn you, so you know what we're dealing with here—" His smile faded and his expression became deadly serious. "I'm pretty sure I'm in love with you already."

"You make it sound like a disaster," she murmured, little bubbles of happiness bursting in her chest.

"It might be, if you don't feel the same way."

She thought carefully, aware that she owed him her certainty. A momentary flood of emotion and a hasty realization might not be strong enough to last a lifetime.

But in the end, she realized the only true answer she could give him was what she felt in her heart.

"I think I'm pretty much in love with you, too," she answered, smiling at the relief in his eyes.

He bent and kissed her deeply, apparently mindless of the fact that they were in a hospital waiting room. "There's got to be a spare broom closet around here," he murmured against her lips. "Maybe the parking deck—"

As tempted as she was to follow him anywhere he wanted to go, she pushed him gently away. "Soon," she promised. "We'll ditch my cousins and find a way to be alone."

The feral look of desire in his eye assured her he would hold her to that promise.

Epilogue

Three months later

When Megan made up her mind, she didn't waffle around. It was just one of thousands of things Evan loved about his brand-new wife.

One of the other things he loved about her was her surprising creativity, he thought with a wicked grin as she whispered her plans for their wedding night into his ear while they danced their first dance as husband and wife.

The wedding had been a simple affair, thrown together with pioneer efficiency by Megan and the other Cooper women, sisters, cousins and in-laws alike. Her two sisters were her attendants, and Del Meade and his family had come to Gossamer Ridge for the wedding, giving Evan a best man who conveniently doubled as the entertainment. Del, Nola and their kids were playing up a storm and everyone seemed to be having a good time.

Megan's mother hadn't been able to get away for the wedding—something about a seminar in Brussels she couldn't get out of. But she'd called to talk to Megan the night before, and she'd sent a lovely antique jewelry chest that might have been a more touching gift if Megan actually wore jewelry.

He closed his hand possessively over his wife's, running his fingertips over the simple gold band on her left ring finger. "When Jesse tries to cut in," he said, "tell him no."

But Jesse wasn't there for a dance. It took one look at his furrowed brow to see that something was up.

"Someone went after Gantry and his family last night," Jesse told them tersely.

"Even with Reid back in jail again?" Evan asked, dismayed.

"Are they okay?" Megan asked.

"Yeah, they got to one of the safe houses we set up near Fayetteville. I talked to Gantry last night."

"You knew this last night and didn't tell us?" Evan asked.

"Didn't want to ruin your wedding with bad news," Jesse replied flatly. "But something else has come up." He nodded toward the side of the banquet hall.

Evan and Megan followed. They found J.D. and Luke Cooper waiting for them, along with her brothers Rick and Wade.

"I asked Gantry if he's been holding out on us," Jesse said. "He admitted there was one thing he'd heard about while he was being jerked around by Barton Reid, something they might want to cover up."

"Which was what?" Megan asked.

"Apparently, Merriwether was right. This is a lot bigger than just Barton Reid."

"We always thought that might be the case," Rick said, "especially with the suspected mole in the CIA."

"Gantry told me he overheard Reid talking to another State Department official about 'three generals,'" Jesse said.

"Three generals?"

"Gantry thinks it might be the three generals who were in charge of the peacekeeping mission in Kaziristan." Jesse lowered his voice.

"General Ross of the army, General Harlowe of the air force and General Marsh of the marines," Luke supplied.

Megan gave her brother an odd look. "Rita's father?"

Jesse's lips flattened to a thin line. "The Marshes aren't currently in the country. I tried calling."

"Maybe they were just screening," Rick said drily.

Jesse gave him a black look. "I checked. General Marsh is in Iraq for the next couple of weeks. I got through to Evie."

Evan glanced at Megan, not following the undertones of the conversation.

"Rita's Jesse's ex-fiancée. Evie's her little sister.

Bad ending to a doomed love affair," she summed up beneath her breath. Apparently not quietly enough if Jesse's dark glare was anything to go by.

"What about General Ross?" J.D. asked.

"That's where it gets interesting," Jesse answered. "General Ross died in a one car crash just three months ago. The police seem to have some questions about the mechanics of the crash, so they haven't entirely closed the case."

"So, maybe someone made him crash?" Megan guessed.

"That's what I'd like to find out," Jesse admitted. "Gantry seems to think the three generals may have been onto whatever conspiracy Barton Reid was part of. That would certainly put them on someone's hit list."

"Why wouldn't they just come clean about their suspicions, then?" Megan asked. "Get it out in the open?"

"If the conspiracy went high enough, they'd have to play it very carefully," Luke answered.

"I made some calls. It looks like Ross's widow lives on a private island down in the Gulf, not far from Terrebonne," Jesse said. "A place called Nightshade Island. She needs help archiving her husband's collections and correspondence, so I called this morning and talked her into letting Cooper Security handle the job."

"Great," Megan said. "Who're you going to send?"

"I haven't decided yet," Jesse said. He smiled at her. "But enough of this mess. It's your wedding day. Dad's looking for his dance."

Megan sighed and looked up at Evan. "Remember what I told you a minute ago?"

He did, vividly. "Yep."

She shot him a saucy grin. "Hold that thought."

JESSE COOPER SPOTTED an uninvited guest lurking near the punch bowl. Glancing around the room to see if anyone else had noticed the stranger, he edged his way across the room.

"Rick knows what you look like," he told his silent partner, Maddox Heller, who was sipping a cup of peach punch and watching the mass of revelers on the dance floor with a bemused smile on his face.

"Rick's too busy looking down his wife's dress to notice me," Heller drawled. He held up his cup. "Good punch."

"I assume you must need something to risk coming here."

Heller met Jesse's gaze, his smoky blue eyes sharp. "Did you decide what to do about the Nightshade Island job?"

"You're right about Gideon Stone. I asked around—he's smart and he's very protective of the Ross family."

"Their son died saving him. A marine doesn't forget that."

"I know. And he'd spot a trained operative a mile away."

Heller took another sip of punch. "So, who'd you choose?"

Jesse looked across the dance floor, where his youngest sister was dancing with his cousin's teenaged son. "The only Cooper who doesn't look like she could hurt a fly."

Heller followed his gaze. His brows quirked with surprise. "You sure?"

Anything but, Jesse thought. But he had to get someone inside the compound on Nightshade Island to find out what kind of secrets the three generals might have uncovered.

Shannon was the best choice. The only choice.

He just hoped he wasn't about to send her into a mess she wasn't equipped to handle.

* * * * *

Look for more books in Paula Graves's COOPER SECURITY *miniseries later in 2012, wherever Harlequin Intrigue books are sold!*

LARGER-PRINT BOOKS!
GET 2 FREE LARGER-PRINT NOVELS PLUS
2 FREE GIFTS!